BIRTHRIGHT

ELIZABETH KNIGHT

CREATIVE WONDER PUBLISHING

Knight, Elizabeth

Birthright

Editing: Swish Editing & Design

Cover artist: Malice and Mayhem Book Covers

Formatting: Creative Wonder Publishing

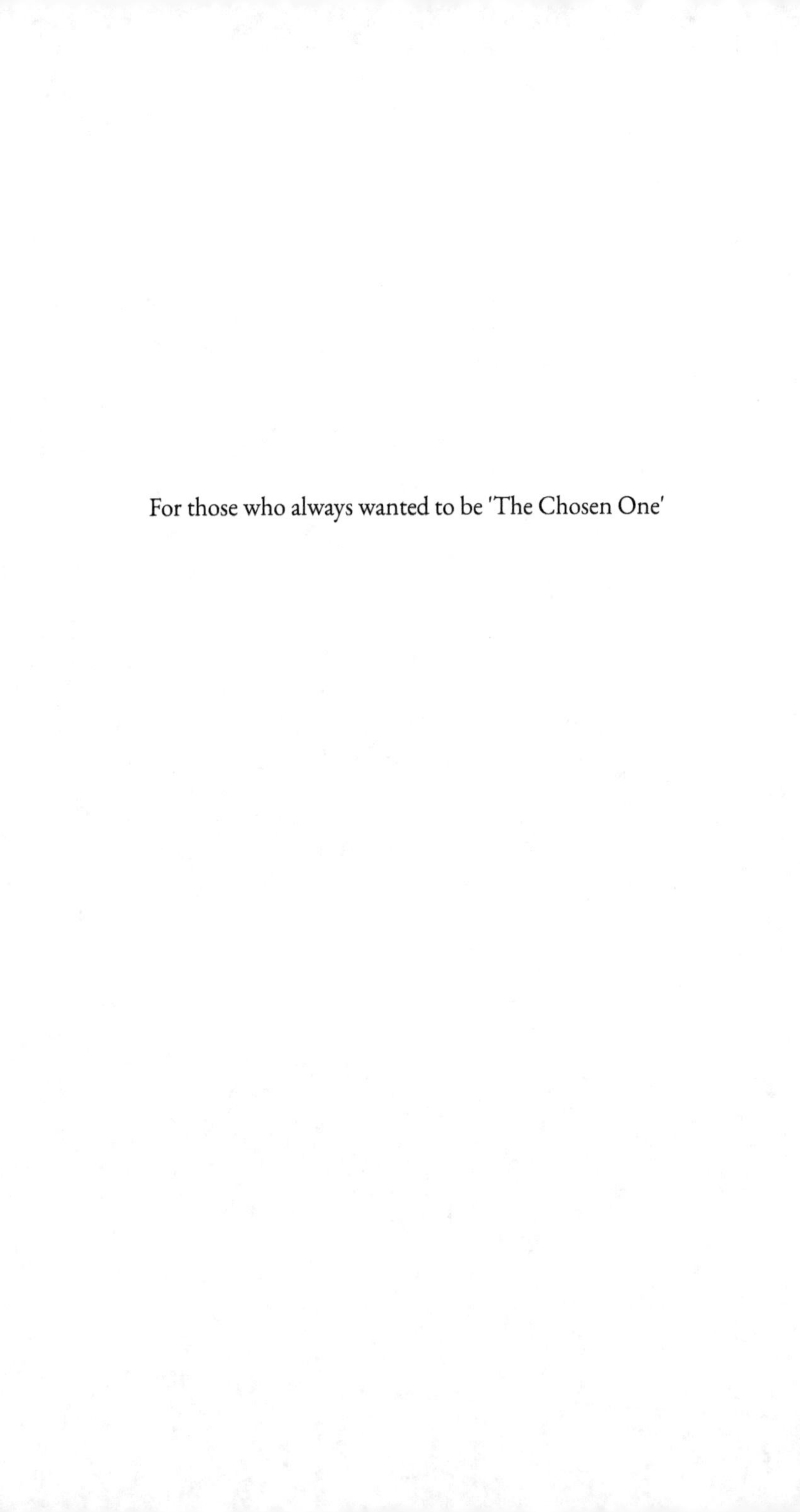

For those who always wanted to be 'The Chosen One'

CONTENTS

BIRTHRIGHT

A particular right of possession or privilege one has from birth, especially as the eldest child.

WELCOME TO COURT

"Cassarah, would you please stop moving, or we will never get you ready in time," my mother snapped.

While I'd let my thoughts wander far from here, I'd all but forgotten the myriad of women running around my room getting me ready. I was finally going to be presented at court later today.

I stood on a small round pedestal in only a white floor-length chemise. I heaved a heavy sigh and frowned at my mother's back as I watched her walk over to grab my corset, also known as my archnemesis. I battled with that thing every day. I was forever grateful I'd missed the fashion era when having the smallest waist was considered beautiful. Mind you, they still didn't like over-indulgent women—hence the corset—but you no longer had to have your waist be the same size as your neck. I quickly swept my thick, curly black hair up and out of the way so it wouldn't get caught in the strings. I knew my mother wouldn't be careful.

I took my last deep breath of the day as the all-too-familiar fit of the corset was wrapped around my waist. I had to place my feet shoulder-width apart so I wouldn't be pulled off the pedestal as they strapped me in. I vowed that someday I would find a way to outlaw the use of these torture devices. There had to be a better way to get the same look without worrying about breaking ribs if it was too tight.

I exhaled as my mother suddenly pulled the string taut. It caused me to grunt at the sudden constriction, and I had to stop myself from glaring over my shoulder at her as my body followed the pull from her brisk action.

"Sorry, Mother, I wasn't ready," I said, grabbing my bedpost to hold myself steady.

"A lady should always be prepared," my mother chided. "Remember... without pain, there is no beauty."

"Who came up with that rule anyway? Why do I have to be in pain to be beautiful?" I mumbled under my breath so my mother couldn't hear. I'd been lucky to avoid her swift skill with a switch thus far today.

"Stop that! It's unbecoming. A true lady always speaks clearly and never complains. We ladies must suffer gracefully in silence."

I sighed. "I've already had my decorum lessons today, Mother."

"Well, clearly it wasn't enough if I still need to remind you how to be a proper lady. We are presenting you in court today. You must be found without a single fault, Cassarah. I will not let your father's tainted blood ruin your chances at marrying up in the world," she reminded me for the millionth time.

"I understand, Mother, but why do I need to worry about getting married when I haven't even been to court?" I countered.

My mother looked at me like I'd just slapped her. "Do you think I haven't been talking relentlessly to the ladies in court to find you a suitable husband?"

"I'm sorry, Mother, I didn't know," I said, gritting my teeth at the idea. "You never mentioned anything to me."

Keep calm! Don't say anything else! Just keep your mouth shut! I told myself as my mind furiously whirled with visions of my mother planning my wedding. And all this before I'd even met the man I was to be stuck with for the rest of my life.

One of the maids draped a full, blood-red skirt over my head, securing it into place. Then she helped me slide my arms into a snug, embroidered black overdress. The overdress had long sleeves and a square neckline that accented my full chest and pale white skin. If I had my way, I would've picked something a little less flashy, but that wasn't an option.

Once I was fully dressed, I was seated on a low stool and then set upon by two women. One worked on taming my hair into some sort of style, and the other worked on placing all my jewelry on.

"It's a mother's duty to her daughter to prepare an advantageous marriage. It shouldn't have to be said," my mother answered as she directed the ladies. "No, not that circlet, the other one. We need to make her copper eyes more noticeable."

"I don't think that's a problem, Mother. They're hard to miss," I interjected.

"We must make the most of each of your assets. This will be your first impression on the king and queen, and I plan on making it one they will never forget." She smiled as she looked over my form.

"Don't you think the fact that you're having me presented late will do that for us?" I asked. "Not many families wait 'til their firstborn is twenty-one."

My mother narrowed her eyes at me to let me know I had crossed the line. *Damn!* I had been doing so well.

"Becka," my mother called.

My handmaid and only friend walked up to my mother, keeping her eyes downcast. "Yes, m'lady?"

Without warning, my mother slapped her hard across the face, leaving behind a perfect red impression of her hand. I flinched, knowing how much that hurt. My heart broke for Becka. If I weren't going to be presented at court today, I would've been the bearer of that welt. Waving Becka away, my mother turned back to me with her thin lips pursed.

"Don't think that because you can't have marks showing on *you* means that I won't demand discipline for your behavior. *This* is exactly why you haven't been presented in court before now. You are far too wild. I blame your father and his tainted blood. I should have never agreed to marry him."

My anger burned at her words. This cold, bitter woman before me was a viper dressed in silk. Try as I might to rein in my tongue and keep my thoughts to myself, I couldn't seem to do it at the moment.

"I'm not some silly little doll you can dress up and parade around for your own benefit," I snapped, giving in to my anger.

"Oh, you poor, silly child... of course you are," she said as she tweaked a few small things into place. "When you get married and have a family of your own, you'll do the same thing for your daughter."

Just then, I heard the clatter of horse hooves on the cobblestone in the courtyard below my bedroom window.

"Looks like we finished just in time," my mother said, clapping her hands to dismiss the maids from the room.

I froze in terror. Being alone with my mother was never good. As much as I wanted to stand up for myself, I'd learned it was always more painful for me to fight back. I watched as my mother glided over with a dangerous look in her eye. I had nowhere to run.

"Cassarah, I don't need to remind you what will happen if this day doesn't go well, do I?" she purred, letting her nails caress my cheek.

"No, Mother," I whispered, accepting my fate.

My mother placed a feather of a kiss on my cheek where I could still feel the bite of her nails. "We will meet you at the palace later, Cassarah."

Becka hurried in once my mother was out of the room and walked over to me. "Are you okay?"

I looked up at my friend's face, still marked with my mother's anger. It was almost as red as her hair and on skin so pale it shone like a beacon. "I should be asking you that. I'm so sorry. I had no idea she would revert to doing that after so many years."

"It's fine. I can handle it," Becka said, giving my hand a reassuring squeeze. "Come on, we shouldn't keep her waiting."

I took one final look in the full-length mirror, then made my way downstairs to the front hall.

"You weren't thinking of leaving before you said goodbye, were you?" my father's deep, rumbling voice called out from behind me.

I looked back in his direction and smiled. I'd always found comfort in my relationship with my father when things with Mother got bad. I thankfully took after him in looks—we shared the same copper-colored eyes and dark curly hair. The only thing I acquired from my mother was her pale white skin. My father had a much darker complexion. He wrapped his strong arms around me and hugged me. He was much taller than me, and my head only reached the middle of his chest.

"Honey, you will ruin her appearance by hugging her so tightly," my mother's sharp tone interjected, cutting our hug short.

My mother was the opposite of my father in every way. She hated displays of affection and scolded him every time it went too far. Her soft blonde hair was always pulled tightly away from her face, hidden by an elegant hair net. Her dark brown eyes always seemed to be moving, watching, and making sure she never made a misstep. When standing next to my father's massive frame, she looked so small and slender. However, I'd learned long ago not to mistake her for being harmless.

"Of course, my flower, I should have known better. I just was so overwhelmed with pride at our beautiful daughter," my father said, gently releasing me and giving me a wink.

My father, for some reason beyond my understanding, loved my mother. Even though he would comfort me after each of my mother's punishments, he never prevented them. I didn't know if it was because she had control over him—just like everything else in her world—or if it was his love that blinded him. I was the only thing in her life she couldn't seem to completely bend to her will, and it wasn't from lack of trying.

"I better get going, I don't want to miss my name being called," I said, winking back at my father, then bowing my head slightly to my mother.

Oddly, they both waved farewell as I rumbled out of the courtyard and onto the open road. My mother was only doing it to show what a perfect family we were to the castle staff.

As we began the hour-long journey to the castle, I let my mind wander to the palace and what was coming next. The king and queen would meet with all of us, gauging if we would be fit material for court life. They would also unlock your family's magical Birthright if you were blessed enough to have one.

Over the years, the wondrous traits that families once possessed had become watered down into nothing more than handy parlor tricks. My mother's family lost their Birthright two generations back, but my father's Birthright had presented him with the ability to never miss a target with his bow.

However, he gave up using the bow entirely almost immediately after his Birthright had manifested. In his eyes, it tied him to our unspoken past, which he was trying to distance himself from. It all seemed terribly silly to me. I thought we should be thanking our ancestors for acquiring such a great honor, but I seemed to be the only one who was proud of what our ancestors had given us.

In the eyes of Norden's nobility, my family had a blemished past. My father's tainted blood, to be specific. His family originated from a clan of mercenaries, a group of hired hands who worked for whoever paid the best price. Somehow, many generations ago, our family had been given the title of 'Baron' and land to go with it. No one really talked about how that came to be, but I knew it wasn't a common practice.

Since we hadn't been born into our title, my family always sought to show how far removed we were from such a distasteful heritage. To compensate for our lack of pedigree, we became skilled in all the proper activities that were befitting of our station. And since I was an only child, I had to be found without fault in all areas.

I looked out the carriage window, wondering if I'd be able to live up to my mother's expectations if I'd be found worthy of the king and queen's acceptance into court. A large shadow was moving across the land, and I looked up to see a dragon flying toward the castle.

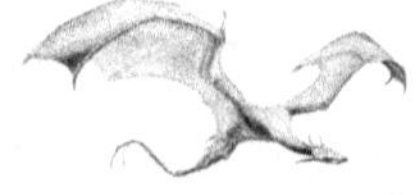

Sometime later, I was awoken by the clamoring sounds of Royal City. I pulled back the heavy velvet curtain and peered out at the bustling streets. The city was full of people working, selling, buying, or just traveling through, like myself.

It was one of the most interesting places I'd ever visited, and I'd only been here twice. That would finally change once I got accepted into court—I'd be required to visit the castle once a week for the first two years of my courtier life to complete my education.

As the carriage rattled over the wooden drawbridge and made its way into the castle's courtyard, page boys scurried out of various areas to come and hold the horses and help me out of the carriage. Once I was out, I shook my skirts, ensuring they hadn't wrinkled too badly on the ride over. My mother would kill me if I had creases everywhere.

I followed one of the pages as he showed me into a sitting room where a few other firstborns were already waiting for the presentation ceremony. Some were playing cards, while others were reading books or looking out the windows at the gardens. Wanting to stretch my legs, I took a turn about the room, pausing here and there to examine things that caught my eye. My nerves grew as I waited, trapped in this stuffy room.

"Did you hear? The crown prince isn't going to be here today," a girl pouted to another she was sitting next to. "How will I get him to notice me if he never shows up to public events like this?"

"I heard his mother is trying to marry him off to one of the neighboring kingdoms threatening our trade treaty," her friend responded, shaking her head.

The pouting girl gasped, covering her mouth with a small, gloved hand. "No, they can't! What about all of us waiting for a chance to be presented to him? It's not fair!"

I rolled my eyes as I left the window I'd been standing in front of and drifted to the other side of the room. I couldn't stand listening to the simpering of a snotty girl who had no idea how the real world worked. If Errit closed the borders to us, this would be a big problem indeed. That's not even mentioning the goods they supplied us with. My skin started to itch with smothered emotion as I tried to keep from getting worked up at things I couldn't change. Finally, I focused on a few girls playing a card game I was familiar with.

"Would you like to join our game?" one of the girls asked. "It might help to keep you from dwelling on our first court appearance."

"Is it that obvious?" I asked, embarrassed I hadn't controlled my emotions better in public, even if it wasn't for the reason the girl assumed.

"If you weren't nervous, that would be most unusual," she stated with a slow blink.

"Then yes, I would gladly join your game," I said, smoothing my expression and arranging my skirts to sit.

Just as I sat, the door opened, and a palace steward walked in and bowed. "The king and queen will see you now. If you would please follow me, I will take you to the throne room."

We all stood and followed him out the door and down the hall, joining with the male firstborns who'd been waiting in a different room. As I looked around, I counted ten of us to meet with their majesties. I didn't really know how many people were usually here for a firstborn ceremony, but I felt this was a small group. I distracted myself by looking at all the beautiful paintings of past royalty and heroes that hung on the walls.

Two guards stationed at the end of the hall pulled open a set of large double doors, revealing a magnificent room adorned with detailed murals depicting angels, flying horses, and what looked to be baby dragons along the walls and ceilings. The room was full of courtiers who watched excitedly as we were led down the center of the room, chatting to each other as we passed, the women hiding behind their fans and gossiping about God knows what.

The king and queen sat on a pedestal in two high-backed chairs made of dark, polished wood. King Edward was regaled in dark blue from head to toe, setting off his fine features. Queen Mary was clothed in golds and creams, contrasting the cascade of red curls around her face. The young man who sat a step down from the queen's left had to be the younger of their two children, Prince Phillip.

"Your Majesties, I present this season's court petitioners," the steward said loudly as he bowed, signaling the rest of us to bow as well.

"Welcome to you all," Queen Mary said, smiling. "We would like to speak to each of you individually so that we might know our new arrivals."

The steward took a few minutes to move us around according to some unknown order before the king's herald called the first name. It was a young man, the son of a duke a few provinces over from ours. They talked with him for a while, asking questions, smiling, and then laughing at something he said. Then they sent him back to stand with us, and the next person was called up. The poor thing looked like she was going to throw up. After her was another young woman who seemed very confident and answered all questions simply and assuredly. There was no doubt she was going to make it in—she was the picture-perfect court lady.

"Presenting Lady Cassarah, firstborn of Baron Charles and Baroness Adeline," the herald announced.

I walked toward them and curtsied low, hovering a moment before standing straight again. I made sure I had proper posture with a slight smile, just as I'd been taught.

"Ah, the firstborn of Baroness Adeline. She is such a dear friend to my younger sister. How is your mother doing, dear?" Queen Mary asked, giving me a genuine smile.

"My mother is doing very well. She is very excited to see you and your sister tonight at dinner," I answered, knowing that was exactly what Mother would want me to say.

The queen chuckled a little at that. "I have no doubt she is very excited to show off her daughter at court, seeing as she's kept you hidden all these years. Tell me, what would she boast about to her friends?"

"My mother would most assuredly tell everyone that I am a graceful dancer as if I float on air," I answered, hearing my mother saying it in my head. "She would also tell you I'm very skilled in needlework, weaving, painting, and poetry."

"Good heavens, child, your mother has been busy with you," King Edward said, laughing. "Tell me what your father has had you learn. I know what an intellect he is."

"My father is a smart man indeed. He has taught me how to speak three different languages and read and write them as well. He says for anyone to get anywhere in this kingdom, they must first be able to understand it. He also taught me arithmetic up to the basics of geometry."

Both the king and queen looked shocked to hear that. Most women in our kingdom could only read and write their name and add basic household accounts. I was proud of what my father taught me. Those were the things I would need to know for the rest of my life, not how to sew a pretty flower on a pillow.

"Well, it seems your family has taken great pains in your education. It also shows how smart you are to learn all these various tasks as detailed as you have said. I think you would be a great asset to the courts," Queen Mary said, holding out her hand to me.

Apparently, the others didn't have Birthrights to be unlocked, which is why they hadn't done this part.

I grasped her hand and held it lightly as I bowed over it, kissing the large black gem set on her ring. "I am honored that Your Majesties would think that of me."

"Welcome to the court, Lady Cassarah," King Edward said, smiling as he touched my shoulders with his scepter.

I waited for something to happen after my Birthright had been unlocked, but I felt no different other than getting a cold chill and goose bumps. I'd passed the test and would be accepted into court.

We all had to wait until the rest had the chance to talk to the king and queen before we could leave. There had been two in the group who hadn't been accepted into court, but the rest of us had, along with our Birthrights unlocked.

The king and queen had just finished accepting the last petitioner when a man burst into the room. The crowd around the throne room dropped into silence as the man skidded to a stop before Their Majesties.

"The dragon's clutch is hatching!"

Two

Dragons

"**S**o soon? I thought we had two weeks to send out invitations to the families," the queen said, sounding worried.

Hatchings were a huge event. Female dragons were rare, and typically, only one or two of them would ever have a clutch of their own. The golden female was the only one who consistently had a clutch, which only happened once every ten years.

When the golden dragon's clutch hatched—usually precisely a year after the eggs were laid—a group of firstborn men and women from surrounding noble families were invited to the event, giving them a chance to bond with one of the hatchlings. Once the baby dragon chose, the two were paired for life.

Apparently, this hatching was happening a little sooner than expected.

"That can't be helped, my dear. Everyone knows that dragons do what they want," King Edward said, patting the queen's arm.

"Very true, My King. We must make the most of what we have." Queen Mary looked around the room as if she were searching for someone. She then leaned over and whispered something in the king's ear, and he nodded in agreement.

King Edward stood and addressed the room. "New firstborn additions to court are invited to the dragon hatching."

I was shocked.

I never thought I would be accepted into court and have the chance to bond with a dragon on the same day. One of the other girls gasped and covered her mouth quickly, knowing that was very unladylike. The boys grinned, patting each other on the back and puffing out their chests.

"Send out messengers to the families that are in the city. Thank goodness dragons take their time getting out of those eggs," Queen Mary said to the steward at her side before she turned her bright green eyes on us. "Follow me as we go to the dragon's nesting area."

Still slightly stunned at the turn of events, the whispers of the people around me faded into the background. As a firstborn, it was never about you—no, it was about getting into court and finding a husband or wife. Yet somehow, I managed to be born and presented to court at the right time to be here when a dragon clutch was hatching early. As we left the throne room and the other court members behind, it finally hit me that this was really happening.

"Now, what do you know about a dragon hatching?" Queen Mary asked the group as we walked briskly down the hall. "Traditionally, we have those chosen tutored in dragon history, but we will have to make do under the circumstances."

"I know that firstborn children of any age can be present if they've never had a chance to be at a hatching," the young woman beside me said.

"Correct. What else?"

"A dragon does not have to bind itself to a human and can choose to be on its own," I said, remembering what little my father had told me.

"Yes. It seems that at every hatching, fewer dragons pick someone, but such is the nature of dragons," Queen Mary confirmed.

"There are six kinds of dragons. The common ones are brown, green, and blue. Then the less common are red and purple dragons, and finally, there is the rare golden queen dragon," a young man piped up.

I started to zone out of the conversation, distracted by all the paintings on the corridor walls. My eye caught one that seemed slightly different than the others. The woman depicted wasn't royalty, or at least she wasn't dressed like one. The woman was dressed in leather and looked more like a warrior. That wasn't what caught my eye, though—it was the fact I felt like I was looking into a mirror. Her amber eyes flashed with determination, and her wild black hair whipped around her head like she was in a windstorm. Trying to take it all in, I stepped on the hem of my dress and tripped, running into one of the other girls.

"Lady Cassarah, is everything okay?" Queen Mary asked.

"Yes, Your Majesty, my foot just slipped from my shoe." Blushing, I made a show of moving my foot around as if putting my slipper back on. "My apologies for causing a stir."

"All is well. I'm just glad you didn't hurt yourself or others," Queen Mary said, believing my little story. "Now we must hurry, or we will miss the whole thing."

With that, we headed off at an even faster pace and dispensed with the talking, exiting through a large wooden door and swiftly walking through a manicured garden. That placed us in view of the dragon roost, the oldest building in the kingdom.

The roost was an impressive structure, but seeing it from afar was nothing compared to walking inside. The rough-hewn stone walls stretched high into the sky and were interspersed with large, arched openings that allowed the dragons to fly inside. Its domed structure was large enough to hold six fully grown dragons—which tended to be about the size of a large draft horse with a twenty-foot wingspan—as well as several hatchlings. In the middle was a sandy arena where the queen's golden dragon was laying, watching over the eight eggs wobbling from side to side. The king's blue dragon was perched in one of the hollowed-out cubbies in the side of the dome, watching over everything.

"You will wait here until I lead you out onto the sand. My dragon will kill anyone who enters the sand without me present," Queen Mary said before she bustled off.

"Can you believe this? We're here at a dragon hatching with a chance to have our very own dragon!" a young man burst out. It seemed as if he'd been holding it in for a while.

"I'm not sure I'm ready for this. I don't know what I would do if I was pair-bonded to a dragon. I have a fear of heights," the young woman beside me said, shivering at the thought. "I think I would be a terrible person to have a dragon."

"What about you? Bet your family will be beside themselves knowing they have a chance to have a daughter who has a dragon," another young man jeered at me. "Not bad for a fake noble's firstborn, wouldn't you say?"

"You know, I do believe that you're great-great-grandfather killed the last duke and took his title," I replied coolly, cocking my head at him. "Tell me, how does that really make us any different?"

The young man looked at me with fury in his eyes, then turned his back, ignoring me. *Point for the more educated fake noble,* I laughed to myself. I might not know exactly where I came from, but knowledge is power, and I was happy to remind them lest they forget.

I redirected my attention toward the dragon and the teetering eggs. The eggs themselves were larger than any other I'd ever seen. They would probably come just past my knee and would almost be too large to wrap my arms around.

"The first egg has cracked," someone called out from a lookout post. "Two eggs have cracked. Three, four, five, six eggs have cracked."

Queen Mary approached us with three other people—two men and one woman—who looked much older than us. "We must hurry now. If the eggs are cracking, then we don't have much time."

The queen brought us out onto the hot sand. I was surprised by this because it was a cooler day for our climate. They must heat the sand somehow to keep the eggs at a consistent temperature. She lined us up in a half-moon a few feet away from the eggs, a safe distance in case any of the hatchlings became violent in their first disorienting moments free from the egg.

The first little dragon to be freed—well, relatively little, being the size of a large dog—was covered in slime and a little confused by its new surroundings. It stumbled around, tripping every few steps as if looking for something or someone. Finally, it headed in the direction of one of the men in our group, and as if the man knew the dragon was looking for him, he ran and picked it up from its most recent spill.

Next came a red dragon that paired itself with the woman who was brought in late. Then a brown dragon hatched, walked up to its mother, and started to feed on the pile of meat left near her. A few moments later, the young woman standing beside me cried out, raced forward, and started beating back a purple dragon attacking a small blue one.

"I've got you, little one. I won't let them hurt you!" she shouted as she punched, kicked, and clawed the baby purple dragon off the blue. Deciding it wasn't worth it, the purple dragon hissed and made its way over to its mother. The newly hatched blue dragon curled up in the girl's lap and started humming loudly. The small crowd of family members in the roost gasped at this event, and the twittering of gossip buzzed off the rock walls.

I looked away from the girl and her dragon to see a green dragon and another brown dragon hatch. Each headed for their mother—only three had paired so far. I looked away from them to the last egg that was shaking violently. Could this last egg be mine? Could I even have a chance at this?

Suddenly, the egg burst open to expose a glistening black dragon. The crowd in the roost gasped and began screaming in fear, rushing for the exit. The black dragon turned its bright golden eyes to me, grabbing me with its gaze. I felt like it was searching my soul, looking for something in me.

Then it found it, and the next instant, I felt as if I was set on fire. I opened my mouth to scream, but nothing came out. I was lost in the swirling heat and pain.

"*I HAVE BEEN WAITING FOR YOU,*" a smooth male voice said.

Finally, the heat cooled, and I was able to breathe again. When I opened my eyes, I found the little black dragon standing in front of me, biting into my left arm.

Once he saw I'd opened my eyes, he let go of my arm and sat in front of me, calmly looking into my eyes. I looked up from his gaze and saw the queen running over to me with terror written on her face. I turned my attention to my arm to see how bad the bite was, but surprisingly, no blood was seeping through the fabric, so it couldn't be that bad.

I would have to take the over-dress off to get a better look at it, but I wasn't too worried about it.

"Lady Cassarah, are you all right?" Queen Mary asked as she crouched by my side in a flurry of fabric. "Lord Everett, your assistance, please."

"I'm fine. He didn't bite me very hard… it just broke the skin," I answered, not understanding why she was so worried.

"We need to get you to a healer right away if there's to be any hope at all," Queen Mary said.

As she helped me to my feet, a towering man with a powerful build approached. His calculating dark brown eyes sized me up as he took a few steps closer to me, invading my personal space and making even the roost feel small.

"Lord Everett is going to take you to the palace healer."

"Really, I'm fine. I don't see the need to go to a healer for this," I said, absently turning away from her to find my dragon. Not liking my answer, Lord Everett tried to use his sheer size to intimidate me, and I was trying not to show it was working.

Queen Mary grabbed me and whispered harshly in my ear. "That was not a request. A baby dragon's bite contains lethal venom. It's their only defense until they grow old enough to breathe fire. A black dragon is bad enough for this kingdom without it killing you."

I felt my face drain as I realized what she'd said. My dragon could have just killed me? Is that what the feeling of fire was a moment ago? How could this be happening to me when things were going so well?

Dumbly, I nodded to the queen and let Lord Everett lead me off the sand and back toward the door. Just as I was about to leave the roost, I heard a crooning sound as if something was crying. I looked over my shoulder and saw my black dragon on the edge of the sand, watching me walk away from him. All the other pair-bonded were still on the breeding grounds with their dragons. One was bathing his dragon, another was feeding her dragon, and the blue dragon and her pair-bond were simply spending time together.

"Should I leave him so soon? All the others are staying with their dragons," I asked, feeling that I would be abandoning him if I left now.

"The others didn't have a black dragon that bit them. You should be writhing in pain. Normally, the venom hits fast and hard," Queen Mary said, looking questioningly between my dragon and me. "Regardless, you must go to the healer quickly."

I looked back at my dragon, trying to tell him with my eyes that I would be right back just as soon as I got my arm looked at. As if he understood, he curled up in a little ball and heaved a heavy sigh. Seeing that I wasn't going to move quickly, Lord Everett picked me up and carried me through the garden.

Three

Bites and Superstitions

Lord Everett roughly dragged me into a room filled with herbs and plants hanging from the rafters. He stomped around the room looking for something or someone before growling in irritation.

"Alto, are you in here? I need you to look at this young woman who just got bit by her own dragon," Lord Everett barked.

"A baby dragon bite, you say? Well, that is serious. You don't get to treat that every day," said a chipper feminine voice from somewhere in the room.

I peered around the space, trying to find the person the voice belonged to, and I didn't have to wait long for the woman to come bustling up to the front. She wore a simple light blue dress with a white apron over it. Her tidy brown hair was pulled back into a bun, showing off her beautifully angled features.

"Well, hello there, I'm Alto, the palace healer," she said, smiling at me.

"I will leave her in your hands," Lord Everett said, bowing to me stiffly before he left the room.

"Let's have a look at you, shall we?" Alto said, leading me over to a simple sheet-covered bed.

I unclasped the overdress and with Alto's help, slipped off the tight sleeves to see my injured arm. We both gasped in shock at what we found. Instead of the bite mark we'd been expecting, I had what looked like a fresh brand, my skin raised in angry red welts arranged in a fractal swirling pattern.

"Well, this is most certainly not a dragon bite," Alto said, her eyes shining with excitement. "I've never seen anything like this before. The good news is that you've clearly not been poisoned and are in no danger of dying."

"I'm thankful for that, truly, but what happened to my arm?" I asked, worried. "How am I going to explain this to my family when they see it?"

"From what little I know of black dragons, they play by their own rules. This could be how he marked you as his pair-bond. That would be my best guess, though I'm not really sure," Alto answered, shrugging her shoulders. "It's been, oh, a hundred years or so since the last black dragon."

I tried to keep up with everything, replaying what happened when my dragon hatched. The voice that echoed in my head, I knew without a doubt, was his. Did all dragons do that? I'd never heard of anyone else being able to hear their dragon talk. Maybe it was a secret they kept to themselves.

"Do dragons speak to their pair-bond?" I asked.

Alto blinked at me, caught off guard by my question. "No, I've never heard of dragons speaking. Did your dragon speak to you?" Alto asked, clutching my hand in hers, eyes wide with excitement.

Not wanting to admit it but knowing I should, I nodded my head once and quickly looked down at the floor, waiting for the reaction.

The room was silent for a few heartbeats, making me want to run back to my dragon.

"What did your dragon say to you?" Alto asked.

"It doesn't really make any sense to me. He said he'd been waiting for me." I looked at her face, searching for answers. "What does that mean?"

"To me, it sounds like you and your dragon have a job to do," Alto said, her face turning serious. "Seems like you're the reason the eggs hatched so early. Your dragon knew you were here in the city and you needed to be present at the dragon hatching. Now let's get you back to him. A newly hatched dragon is not very friendly to anyone but its pair-bond." She glanced once more at my forearm before I put my overdress back on.

We made our way back to the roost in silence, neither one of us knowing what to expect once we got there. A small crowd was still milling around the outside, talking about the hatching and the strange events that happened. Once they saw me, I could feel their furtive glances, and I tried to ignore the gossip, entering the roost to find my hatchling.

But I didn't see anyone in the hatching area or surrounding alcoves. I couldn't even find my dragon.

"I don't see my dragon anywhere. Would they have taken him somewhere?" I asked an attendant.

"It's here somewhere. It'd be most unusual for someone, even another pair-bond, to interact with another's dragon," the attendant answered.

Just as I was going to search deeper in the roost, I heard a loud, hissing snarl coming from deep in one of the alcoves. I raced over to the other side of the hatching ground, instinctively knowing it was my dragon making that sound. I was filled with panic—I had no idea what was going on, but I could feel his pain and anger.

I halted in front of the opening and gasped at what I saw. My dragon was crouched in the back of the alcove, cornered by three guards with spears trained on him. Blood seeped out of the wounds that covered his body, where their spears had already pierced his skin.

Anger welled up in me at this outrage. What right did they have to harm my dragon?

"What do you think you are doing to my dragon?" I demanded.

One of the guards looked at me in surprise. "You're still alive?"

"Of course I'm alive. Why would you think otherwise?"

"Lord Everett said your dragon bit you. We couldn't let your dragon live if his pair-bond was killed. They go crazy when that happens."

"Did he go crazy before you started jabbing at him with your spears?"

"No... he was sleeping," he answered, his unease growing.

"Then why, might I ask, did you feel the need to corner my dragon and kill him?"

"I ordered them to," a voice boomed from behind me.

I whipped around to see Lord Everett.

"Too bad your dragon didn't take care of killing you. Now I'll have to deal with you as well. It truly is fitting that a person of your lineage would end up with a cursed dragon. Yet another mark against your family that is trying so hard to hide their past," he said, letting his disdain for me drip from every word.

How had I missed this hatred when he'd brought me to the healer? My guess was the only thing that had kept him from killing me then was the queen's command.

"What does any of this have to do with my family?" I asked, my anger pushing aside my fear of him.

He chuckled a little before he answered. "Everything, you stupid girl. Did they teach you nothing?"

He knew full well my family never spoke of our ancestors. He was just saying this to anger me. "Feel free to explain to me what that's got to do with you killing my dragon."

"The black dragon is an abomination," he snarled, "and should be disposed of swiftly before it can work its evil magic." He looked past me at his three men, watching our exchange. "What are you staring at? Finish the job." Then he turned back to me. "I'll deal with you myself."

Anger flooded my body at that statement. *Who was he to decide if I should live or die?*

Lord Everett shoved me into the alcove, almost knocking me over. I stumbled a few steps and found my feet again, trying to come up with some way to keep this man from killing me. Lord Everett drew his sword and marched toward me as I backed closer to my dragon.

I had no way to defend myself or my hatchling. I was helpless. Nothing I'd been taught for the past twenty-one years would be of any help to me now.

Taking a deep breath, I gathered what little courage I had and screamed as loud as I could. When I ran out of breath, I screamed again and again. Lord Everett stopped with his arms still raised in readiness, but the other men dropped their spears and took off, not wanting to get caught. I tried to hold onto the courage that was quickly fleeing away with the look of contempt that Lord Everett directed my way.

"I will not let you kill me or my dragon! You have no right to do so. If I have to draw the whole kingdom here with my screaming, I will," I said resolutely, backing up the rest of the way until I shielded my dragon.

"Go ahead and scream all you want. They won't get here in time," he answered, advancing and raising his sword above his head. "How nice. I can end both of you with the same stroke of my sword."

Just before he was going to slice deep into my chest, I instinctively thrust my hands out, and an arrow buried itself into his shoulder. Lord Everett dropped his sword and began spewing vulgar obscenities.

"Who shot me?" he yelled, looking around. Then he turned and frowned at me. "You did this to me? Where did you even get that bow?"

I looked down at my outstretched arm and blinked a few times, making sure I wasn't seeing things. In my left hand was a bright, glowing bow, intricately designed and lighter than air. The pattern on the bow reminded me of something that I'd seen before, but I couldn't quite place it. I tried to drop it, but when I released my hand, it vanished into thin air as did the arrow in Lord Everett's shoulder.

"It seems we now know what your Birthright is, Lady Cassarah," King Edward's voice said calmly from behind Lord Everett.

I shifted slightly to see the king and queen standing a few steps away with guards. I tried to recover from my shock and bowed to them, not sure what else to do in this situation. *Did they agree with Lord Everett? Were they going to sentence me to death?*

"Lord Everett, I demand an explanation!" King Edward barked, his cool blue eyes trained on his captain. "I certainly don't remember ordering you to harm this dragon or his pair-bond."

"I was only doing my duty trying to protect the kingdom from this evil dragon's curse," Lord Everett answered, bowing his head.

The queen walked up to me, brushing past Lord Everett to place her hands on my arms and look me in the eye. "Are you all right, my dear? I heard you scream, and we both came running as fast as we could."

"I am unharmed, Your Majesty, but I can't say the same for my dragon," I answered, a little shaken at what had just happened.

"Get that arrow wound looked at, and I don't want to see you near the roost or this dragon ever again. If that should happen, you will not just be stripped of your position. Know that harming a paired dragon without just provocation is punishable by death," the king said coldly.

"As Your Majesty commands." Lord Everett grunted as he left.

I turned slowly to my dragon curled up in the corner, still breathing heavily. I kneeled beside him and gently started to examine his wounds. Some were deeper than others, but all of them were bleeding.

I turned back to the king and queen, tears welling up in my eyes. "Do we have healers for dragons?"

"We do, but he was called away from the roost to heal a dragon in another city. We thought we had another few weeks before the eggs hatched, and he was to be back by then," Queen Mary answered.

"We need to do something for him, or else he's going to bleed to death. Is there anyone else who can help me?" I begged, feeling tears roll down my cheeks.

"The dragon healer does have an apprentice. He's the only other one in the city who knows anything about healing dragons. I will send someone to fetch him," Queen Mary said before leaving.

Not caring what the king would think of me, I sat on the sandy ground of the alcove and lifted my dragon's smooth, scaled head into my lap. I gently stroked his head, just like I did for the cats in our home, and soon I felt a humming against my leg. As I continued, his breathing eased, and he seemed to be able to rest. I heard the king's footsteps as he walked over to us, but I only had eyes for my dragon. As if my dragon knew the king was there, he paused in his humming to let out a warning growl deep in his throat.

"Don't worry, I'm not here to harm you or your pair-bond," King Edward said reassuringly. "It seems you two have quite the connection already. I've never seen a dragon take to his pair-bond so fast."

I knew the bond I had with this little black dragon would be until death, but the depth of what I felt surprised me. I'd never stood up to my mother, never defended myself the way I should have, yet the thought of someone hurting my dragon gave me this uncontrollable need to protect him at all costs.

As if my dragon heard what I was thinking, one of his golden eyes opened and stared up at me. "*THIS BOND WE SHARE IS STRONGER THAN ANY OTHER YOU WILL EVER KNOW. MOST PAIR-BONDS DON'T ACCEPT THE CONNECTION AS QUICKLY AS YOU HAVE. THEY FEAR IT, AND AS A RESULT, THEY NEVER KNOW THE MANY GIFTS AND BLESSINGS THAT CAN HAPPEN. DON'T FRET, CASS. I WILL BE FINE. DRAGONS HEAL QUICKLY, EVEN MORE SO IF THEIR PAIR-BOND IS WITH THEM.*"

Upon hearing my dragon use my name, it dawned on me that I hadn't given him a name. While we waited for the healer's apprentice, I thought through all of the different languages that I knew, searching for the perfect name. Finally, it came to me. It seemed so simple, and yet it was perfect.

"My little dragon, I've thought of a name for you. Vasin. It means 'kingly.' That way no matter what anybody else says, you'll know how I see you," I whispered softly.

Vasin started humming again. This time it was louder than before as if to show how much he liked his name. Moments later, the healer's apprentice walked into the alcove and kneeled beside Vasin, gently examining his wounds.

"I think he will be just fine. I will place some ointment on the wounds to keep them from getting infected, but they will heal in a day or two," he assured me.

"Thank you so much for looking at him and setting my mind at ease," I said, smiling gratefully at him. "I guess I've got a lot to learn about dragons."

"I'm sure you'll learn fast. If you have any questions, I would be happy to help," he said, giving me a shy smile.

I nodded in agreement but was distracted by a steward who came walking into the alcove. It was then that I noticed the queen was there, watching from just outside the alcove.

"Your Majesty, Lady Cassarah's mother and father are looking for her," the steward said, bowing.

"Is it dinnertime already?" she asked. The steward nodded his head in response and waited. "Tell the Baron and Baroness I'll have her sent over soon. Put them in the private drawing room. Their daughter has much to tell them."

As the steward departed, I looked over at the apprentice, who was swiftly applying salve to Vasin's wounds. "Do you think it's all right for me to just leave him here?"

The apprentice paused in his work and looked at the dragon resting peacefully in my lap. "I think he will be perfectly fine if you are not here with him, but with the connection between you two, neither of you will like the feeling of being apart."

Queen Mary walked over to me and rested her hand on my shoulder. "I know what it feels like to leave your dragon so soon after being paired together, but it will only be for tonight. You are more than welcome to come back to the roost whenever you please. Though I must ask you to come with me now so we can get you changed and ready for dinner."

I nodded, acknowledging the queen's words but didn't move right away. I bent over and hugged Vasin's cool, scaled head. "I'll be back, and I promise nothing bad will happen to you tonight."

"I will have a guard posted at the entrance to this alcove to make sure no one harms your dragon," Queen Mary said, bowing her head to me slightly so I knew how much she meant it.

"Thank you," I said as I stood up from Vasin, then slowly walked out of the alcove and away from my dragon.

Mother Knows Best

"Cassarah!" my mother screeched. "You're filthy! And your dress is covered in dirt and sand! Has nothing I taught you managed to stay in that simple brain of yours?"

I bowed my head, taking the harsh words she sent my way. I really wasn't hearing anything she said, anyway. All I could focus on was the hollow feeling deep in my chest. This must be what the apprentice meant about not liking being apart from Vasin.

My attention was snapped into focus as I felt the lingering sting of a slap across the cheek. I finally looked up from the ground to meet my mother's furious eyes with my murderous gaze.

Keep it together, Cassarah. You just need to let her be mad. Don't piss her off even more. It never goes well in the end.

"How could you do this to your family? After all we've done to get you accepted into court and proper society. You have ruined any chance of marrying a noble! Who would want to marry the woman pair-bonded to the black dragon?" she said, shaking with anger.

A spark lit inside of me at her words. Typically, I would hang my head and let my mother cut me open with her words, but not this time. I was not going to let her speak that way about my pair-bond. She could do whatever she wanted to me, but I would never let her speak ill of Vasin.

"Did I ever say that I wanted to be married?" I barked back, furious that I was being blamed for something I had no control over. "No, Mother. You can't blame this on me, not this time. I never wanted the court life... you did. Furthermore, that black dragon is not a blight on our name any more than you are."

Another slap on the same cheek was my mother's answer. She stood there glaring at me, her chest heaving with anger. "Clearly, you have dealt with a large shock today and will need to be taken home as soon as possible."

Turning her back to me, she signaled to one of the maids. "Please inform the queen that we will be unable to attend dinner this evening due to Cassarah's condition."

"Mother, what are you doing? I'm fine, and I don't need to be sent home like some disobedient child."

"I will not show my face at court with you by my side while you're paired with that creature. I have dealt with the looks and the gossiping behind my back for years because of marrying your father. I will not endure more because of my daughter. I just can't do it," Mother answered, still not looking at me.

"There is nothing I can do to change the fact I am paired. It's a lifelong bond," I said, trying to get her to understand I couldn't just walk away from this.

"Then you will just have to learn to live as if you've never had a pair-bond. I forbid you from seeing that *thing* ever again." With that, she flung open the door and marched down the hall.

"Lady Cassarah, the carriage is waiting," Becka said as she draped my cloak around my shoulders, pulling the hood up to cover my face.

Slowly, I followed Becka as she led the way to the carriage. Mother's words replayed in my mind repeatedly as I tried to figure out what had just happened. Never had I seen my mother express so much emotion before. She was always the cold, proper woman.

As I stepped into the carriage, I felt a stabbing pain in my chest, causing me to gasp. Would it kill me to be taken away from my dragon? As the carriage began its rattling journey out of the palace courtyard, I heard a pain-filled wail come from the direction of the roost. Vasin was feeling the same pain I was. I then began to panic, wondering if this could harm him somehow since he was already so weak.

"Mother, we have to go back. I can't leave Vasin yet... he's wounded," I pleaded, a sense of panic growing in my chest.

I made to jump out of the carriage door, but my mother grabbed a handful of hair and yanked me back. The footman she had strangely asked to ride with us pulled me down to sit next to him, blocking my way to the door and keeping hold of my arm.

"What was that, dear?" Mother asked as if she hadn't heard me.

"Stop it, Mother. You know exactly what I'm talking about. I think it might kill him for me to leave him while he's still wounded," I shot back, frustrated.

"It's better if the thing dies. Then we won't have to worry about it anymore. It's really doing us a favor," she said, looking out the window.

"If he dies, there is a chance that I might die as well. Our pair-bond is so strong that one cannot live without the other for very long."

"Don't be so foolish... you've only just met the thing. There is no way your so-called pair-bond could be that strong already. Now drop the matter before I start your punishment now," she said, ending the discussion with a firm look.

As we traveled further from the castle, the pain in my chest subsided to a dull ache that radiated through my entire body. I tried to sleep on the ride home, but I was unable to, kept awake with worry for Vasin.

Could I survive being away from him forever? I'd never heard of someone who was forced away from their dragon. Most of the time, it was an honor to have a pair-bond, but it would seem this was not the case for me.

My thoughts drifted from Vasin to the strange events that had occurred with Lord Everett. Why would he go behind the king's back to kill my dragon and me? I know he said the black dragon was a bad omen, but what would possess him to act on his own?

Furthermore, how had I managed to shoot him with that arrow? My Birthright was more powerful than any I remembered hearing about. Was it because I'd pair-bonded with a dragon? Could this be the original manifestation of our family's Birthright? I would need to sneak into Father's office and look at the books he kept hidden there. If I couldn't find anything, I'd just have to make him tell me. It seemed our past was not meant to be forgotten quite yet.

"Cassarah!" Mother's sharp voice demanded, pulling me back to the present.

Seeing we were home, I silently followed after her, keeping my head down in hopes she would forget my presence. Father, who'd been riding alongside the carriage, fell into step beside me, letting me know with his presence that he was not upset with me. I truly felt he was the one person who understood me and could ease my troubles. I didn't know how he was going to help in this situation, but I knew he would try to lessen my punishment. Without even being told, I went straight up to my room and got ready for bed. I just wanted this day to be over.

Try as I might, I couldn't seem to fall asleep. Every position seemed to be uncomfortable for one reason or another. Finally, I gave up on sleeping and slipped on my dressing gown, then walked out to the balcony, hoping the cool night breeze would calm my mind. I took a deep breath and looked up at the brilliant twinkling stars in the black sky.

I let my thoughts drift to the dull pain that tied me to my dragon back in the roost. Could he still hear my thoughts from this far away? Deciding to give it a try, I touched the painful feeling and then listened intently to see if I could hear anything in response. As I stood silently in the moonlight listening for my dragon, I felt a slight tug in my chest, as if he was answering my call. Then, as I tried to respond to him, I was overcome with dizziness, and a moment later, I was swallowed up in darkness.

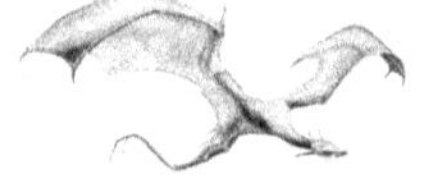

"Cassarah, what are you doing sleeping out on the balcony?" Becka asked worriedly as she shook me awake.

I groaned as I sat up, my muscles punishing me for sleeping on the stone floor. How had I ended up sleeping out here? Try as I might, I couldn't seem to remember anything from last night after I crawled into my bed. Then the memories of what had happened yesterday came flooding back. I was pair-bonded to a black dragon, and my mother was planning on locking me away.

"You really need to get ready for breakfast. You know how your mother hates to be kept waiting," she fretted.

"I know all too well about that, Becka," I grumbled as I walked past her into my bedroom. "Can't say I'm excited to find out what punishment she has cooked up for me."

"We'll get through it, just like we always have. I have some healing herbs in my chambers so I can treat your wounds when she's done," Becka whispered as she filled a ceramic bowl with hot water for me to wash my face and hands.

While I was cleaning up, she went to the closet and picked an outfit for the day, then laid it out on the bed. After I was dressed, I sat on a low stool so Becka could begin the process of taming my hair. After the many years we'd been together, she knew a few tricks about getting it to behave. Once I was presentable and ready for the day, I made my way down the large staircase to the dining room.

A large wooden table that could seat about twenty people was the room's central feature. I'd never seen the table filled with that many people in my life, but just in case, we were ready. I never could understand why my mother insisted we eat every meal there. Yet there she was, seated at one end of the table while Father was at the other. I quietly sat at my place in the middle between the two of them. Good thing my mother hated to talk during meals—it would have been difficult for any of us to hear each other.

"Cassarah, you will need to write a letter to the queen asking for her pardon for leaving so suddenly. Also, include that you are going abroad and cannot attend court for a season," Mother said as the dishes were taken away. "Oh yes, and that you are flattered she is adding you to the list of women considered for the prince's hand in marriage."

"I'm going abroad?" I asked, stunned she would go to such lengths to keep me from Vasin.

"Of course not, but it's the only explanation we can give for you not being at court for a while. Most of the young ladies go abroad once they enter court, so she will not think twice about it."

"Did you also say she has spoken to you about me being wed to the prince? Which prince?"

"Prince Gavin, of course," Mother sniffed.

Before I could address this further, Father cut in.

"Dear, don't you think this is a little much? I mean, lying to the queen could be considered treason, especially if she is being considered. What if someone sees her here at home and not abroad?"

"She will be locked in her room. No one will see her, and I've already explained to the staff that they will be dismissed if they breathe a word of her still being here," Mother said simply. "Besides, she won't want to be seen in the bridle anyway. That will guarantee to keep her out of sight."

As if in reflex, I shot out of my chair and gaped at my mother. "You can't intend to use that vile thing on me again. I haven't done anything in years to deserve that kind of punishment."

"You know very well what you have done, and until you no longer recognize your pair-bond to that abomination, you will stay locked up. Am I clear? Unless you need me to up the punishment?" she said coolly, piercing me with her steady gaze.

"There is nothing I can do to change the fact I am pair-bonded with Vasin. It's a lifelong deal. Not something I can just wish away because you ask me to," I shot back and then turned to look at my father for help.

He looked down as soon as I caught his gaze, bending to my mother's orders. I was on my own—no one was going to help me out of this situation. I turned sharply on my heel and fled the dining room before I made things worse. An hour later, my mother walked into my room with my humiliation in her hands. I could feel my body burn with anger at her doing this to me. One of our stablehands was also with her, holding a thin riding crop.

"Are you going to make this easy?" Mother asked.

I lifted my chin and squared my shoulders. Mother sighed, held out her hand for the crop, and nodded her head to the stablehand. He grabbed me around the waist and tossed me on my bed, then wrapped me tightly in a blanket. The man held onto me as Mother bolted the leather harness over my face. It fit snugly, the leather covering my mouth keeping me from opening my jaw.

I fought to keep still as she started the second part of my punishment. The first sting of the crop on my bare feet made me cry out. With the bridle on, my cries were muffled and contained in this one room. The lashes continued, and I lost count of how many Mother slashed across my feet, but I knew they would be bleeding.

She planned this to make sure I couldn't walk on them for days after. It would be one of the only things that would keep me from trying to run.

When she was done, the stablehand released me, my face buried in the bedding. I felt Mother brush a hand down my head before she left the room, leaving me to my humiliation.

The following days seemed to drag on forever with no end in sight. I was kept in the bridle for five days solid, unable to eat, drink, or speak to anyone around me. After I was freed from that, I was still locked in my room and only let out for evening meals, the only meal I was consistently allowed to eat. Throughout the day, I had class after class in every area that my mother felt I was lacking in. That turned out to be all of them—etiquette, dancing, poetry, needlepoint, painting, and memorizing the most prominent families in the kingdom down to the second cousin. Only now when I didn't get things right, I was whipped with a switch on the palms of my hands or the back of my legs.

By the end of the second week, I felt like I was almost at my breaking point. If I had to practice my curtsies one more time or write another sonnet, I was going to go mad. My only solace in all of this was that my father insisted I keep up my education with him.

The library had become my lifeline. As soon as I entered the dim, oil lamp-lit room, I could breathe a sigh of relief.

Slowly, I developed a plan to get out of here, but my plans to be free of this life of drudgery and abuse were thwarted at every turn. Each time I finally managed to get a maid or teacher on my side, they were dismissed the next day. I could never figure out how my mother knew, but she always found out. Even Father was tight-lipped and unwavering in the situation. She even went so far as to place male servants by the two exits at night to keep me from running away.

As much as I needed to run away from home, I didn't know the first thing about surviving alone out in the world. I'd lived a sheltered life and had no skills that would be of any use in keeping myself alive. I read tons of books about how to live off the land and how to hunt and fish, but mental knowledge was not what I needed.

Day after day, a sense of defeat built as each glimmer of hope was crushed. The punishments became more frequent since I had given up caring about anything. The hollow ache in my chest of missing Vasin was the only reminder of why I needed to stay alive.

One night, unable to fall asleep after three weeks of being trapped in my room, I threw back the covers and started to pace. I was surprised I had the energy, having had my food portions cut in half the past week. When stalking the length of my room didn't help, I decided to see if reading would calm my mind. Silently, I slipped past Becka—who made a show of locking me in my room each night before stealthily unlocking my door—and padded down the hall, then down the servants' stairway to the first floor. Creeping past the servants' sleeping quarters next to the kitchen, I raced down the short hall and into the library. I sighed, proud that I'd made it with no one the wiser.

Taking one of my favorite books off the shelf, I huddled in a corner near the window to read by moonlight. At some point, I must have dozed off because the next thing I knew, I was awoken by the sound of the window next to me opening. I curled up into a little ball, thankful my dressing gown was a dark navy blue and wouldn't be easily seen. I kept as silent as I could as four men dressed in all black entered the library through the window.

They looked like liquid shadows as they arranged themselves around the room. Only one of them seemed to stay out in the open as if waiting for something to happen. Then a few moments later, the library door opened, and Father walked in holding a shrouded candle.

What was going on?

FIVE

GREAT ESCAPE

Huddled deep in the shadows, I watched the scene before me by the dim light of my father's candle. I could now see the leader more clearly. He was older, his dark hair graying, and his face was weathered and stern. His gaze was trained on my father, and I shivered slightly as if I could feel his gaze pinned on me as well.

"Good, you got my note," the older man said, his voice just above a whisper.

"How could I have missed it when you pinned it so carefully into my saddle with your dagger?" Father replied, anger coating his words.

"I needed to make sure you saw it and listened to what it said."

Father grunted at this and glared at the man, unafraid. What was happening? Who were these men, and how did they know my father?

"Why are you here? I thought the clan disowned my family many generations ago when we took the title," Father asked.

"The black dragon has reappeared. That changes everything," the man said simply.

"She knows nothing. I have kept all knowledge of the clan from her as my father should have done with me."

"Your father was wise to teach you of your heritage, even if you have forsaken our ways. But we cannot let that happen to the girl. We need her, and she needs us. Without the clan's protection, she and her dragon will be in danger. We've already heard of the attempts on her dragon's life from our spies at the castle."

"I can protect my child without your help."

The man in black shook his head. "Could we at least speak to her and see what she has to say?"

"No. We will handle this like the noble family we are."

"Who are you to forbid me from talking to her? We of the clan have more claim to her than you do as her father. The black dragon has chosen her as clan queen. The old ways overrule all things, even blood ties."

"Damn you, Ballard. The old ways don't apply to us since we are no longer clan. Once ties are broken, it cancels all obligations to follow the clan's laws. I will not hand over my only child to you!" Father snapped, shaking with anger.

"There is a plan to kill her dragon tomorrow night. If he dies, so will she. Does that change your mind at all?"

"This king would never allow someone to kill a dragon, even if it is a cursed black one."

"The king's own captain of his personal guard has plotted to kill the dragon in order to save the kingdom from its darkness," Ballard hissed.

"Come now. The king has to know about the plan, then. If he makes the call to kill the dragon before it becomes a threat, who am I to stop him?"

"He has planned the attack but won't be there in person. His plan is to make it look like zealots of the church broke into the roost and killed it. It's been taught in the history books that the black dragon is a symbol of death, sickness, and evil." Ballard shifted his weight, pointing a finger at my father. "You know the truth, even if you deny it. That dragon represents change, the darkness before the light can be seen. You're telling me you would sacrifice your child out of misguided prejudice?"

Father rubbed his face with his hand, groaning. "Let's say I let you talk to her and save her dragon. What would you want in return?"

"We would take her to the clan and train her to be our queen," Ballard answered without so much as blinking.

"You're out of your bloody mind if you think I'm going to let that happen! I would be marked a traitor to the kingdom if I gave the mercenaries back their royalty."

Ballard advanced on my father so they were face to face. "You're a fool, Charles! You would rather stand by and let your daughter die than deal with who you really are?"

"Fuck you, you bastard. Get out of my house and never come back here, or I will kill you and any other clan member I find," Father snarled, shoving Ballard away from him.

"Know that her blood is on your hands," Ballard said before he signaled to the others and slipped back out the window.

My father muttered to himself, blowing out his candle as he left the library, leaving me in the dark with more questions than I knew what to do with.

Slowly, I stood, looking out the library window long after the men had left.

What did they mean about the old ways? Did the black dragon really mean I was to be their queen? They must be mental...

But could they be right about the attack on Vasin?

I couldn't take the chance. I had to get out of this house tonight and save him.

I quickly returned to my bedroom, quietly opening the door and slipping past Becka, still sleeping. I smiled down at her. After all the years that we'd been together, I thought of her as a sister. She'd been through it all with me—my temper tantrums and the punishments that happened after, my broken heart when my first crush was betrothed, and everything else in between.

It would be hard to leave her behind without an explanation, but the fewer people who knew where I was going, the better. I couldn't let anyone else take the blame for my running away.

I walked out onto the balcony to take in the view I loved shining in the full moonlight. Closing my eyes, I took in a deep breath, reveling in the feeling of purpose followed by nervous excitement. When I opened them again, I was looking into a pair of deep green eyes shining with mischief. I stepped back, letting out a little squeak of surprise as he climbed over the railing onto the balcony.

"Who are you?" I demanded once I recovered from my shock. "How did you get up here?"

"I climbed," he said, shrugging his shoulders. "A manor this old and neglected is easy to sneak into."

"Why are you here sneaking into my room at all?" I asked, clutching my dressing gown around myself.

I'd heard stories of men creeping into young maidens' rooms and stealing their virtue before they were married.

"I saw you hiding in the library, little mouse."

When I stared at him with my mouth gaping like a fish, he continued, "My grandfather sent me to fetch you. You know, the man who was talking to your father a little bit ago? We can't leave here without you," he said, giving me a dangerous grin. I raised an eyebrow at this strange man's boldness, yet I was still frightened of him.

"I have no idea what you're talking about," I said, turning my back to him and walking into my room.

He quickly grabbed my arm and yanked me back onto the balcony so forcefully that I groaned a little as my back hit the stone railing. He kept himself a handbreadth away from me as he towered over me, pinning me with his fierce gaze. I could feel his warm breath on my face as I looked deep into his fierce green eyes.

"Don't you think I should know your name if we are going to be this well acquainted?" I asked, my voice a little too breathy for my liking.

Why does that matter if he is going to kidnap me? He is rather handsome up close. Stop it! Pull yourself together! Just because he's handsome doesn't mean he can be here in your bedroom.

His intense expression lightened a little at this, and the corner of his mouth turned up in a rueful smile. "Forgive me for not properly introducing myself sooner, but we have more important things to talk about. However, since you are asking for it specifically, my name is Cole, grandson to Ballard, the Regent of the Royal Raven Rose mercenary clan."

I was taken aback by how his gentle expression didn't match the snide words coming out of his mouth. *Who was this guy, really? Does he even know himself?*

"Is there a reason you are still this close to me? As you can tell, I'm not going to fight back, nor could I, even if I wanted to," I said, trying to be as calm as I could while my heart was pounding in my chest.

The feel of his body heat against mine out in the cool air had my skin tingling. His sharp citrus and pine scent surrounded me. It was intoxicating. I'd never been this close to a man before, and my treacherous body was deciding it was kind of okay with it.

"Does a man need a reason to be this close to a pretty lady in her nightgown on a cold night?"

I blushed hotly, dropping my gaze. I'd forgotten I was indeed still only in my night clothes and dressing gown. Glancing down, I noticed my dressing gown had opened when he grabbed me, so he could see the rosy color of my nipples peaked by the chill and his proximity. This was *so* highly inappropriate and one of the most unladylike things I'd ever done. Slowly, I pulled my gown around me, trying to act like I wasn't going to melt in embarrassment.

Who was this man to think he could just show up here and act this way toward a proper lady? Why did I feel that every word he said to me was a veiled threat? Why did that make my heart beat faster?

"Clearly, the man addressing this lady isn't a gentleman because a gentleman would never have climbed into my room. And a true lady would never entertain anyone less than a gentleman," I answered, trying to put some force behind my words. "Besides this being highly inappropriate, if we get caught by Becka, your whole plan will fall apart."

He bent down even closer so I could almost feel his lips on my ear and whispered, "I'm no gentleman, and you're no proper lady. So I suggest we be very quiet and not get caught."

A shiver ran down my spine at the feel of his breath on my neck, then, reacting out of instinct, I shoved him away with all my strength. Unprepared for my assault, he stumbled back a few steps and looked at me, stunned. I wonder if any woman had rejected his advances before, but I wasn't just any woman.

"I would ask that you never do that again," I said, squaring my shoulders and lifting my chin just like I'd been taught to do when speaking to someone of a lower class. "We are not that well acquainted, and you have taken liberties you shouldn't."

Cole examined me for a moment as if he were really looking at me for the first time. He smiled and bowed at the waist flamboyantly. "I beg your forgiveness, My Queen. I never meant to offend you. I will be more careful from now on not to take any liberties with you."

My eyes narrowed at his flippant words. "You dare to mock me right now?" I asked, feeling my temper beginning to rise even higher.

Upon hearing my response, Cole glanced up at me to see if I was being serious. When he saw my expression, he stood up and looked me in the eyes, the friendly mask falling away. "Well, I'm glad to see that our soon-to-be queen isn't a little mouse, after all. This was all a test. I wanted to see if you were a person who is easily swayed by sweet words."

Angry at my emotions being manipulated by this man and now seeing his true nature, I was done talking. I'd had just about all I could deal with tonight, and if pushed again, I couldn't be held accountable for my actions. Mustering up all the good ladylike manners I had left at this point, I tried to make my exit.

"It's late, I'm tired, and I would love nothing else than for this conversation to be over. Besides, I'm planning on saving Vasin myself, so your help isn't needed. So if you could step aside, I'm going into my room and closing the door behind me."

"Is that right? All by yourself? That would be a big feat for a little mouse."

I brushed past him, trying to shove him to the side, but he grabbed my shoulder to stop me once again from entering my room. I swung around, slapping his hand away from me, and the next moment, I was holding that glowing bow of pure energy, nocked and drawn. Upon seeing the bow, he took a few steps back, holding up his hands in surrender.

"Now would not be a good time to make me even angrier," I said in a calm, steady voice.

"So it's true. You do possess the ancient Birthright of queens past. I have no choice but to acknowledge that you, of all people, will become our queen." With that, he kneeled, bowing his head.

"Why do you keep going on about me being a queen? I am the farthest thing from a queen." I huffed.

Cole looked up at me. "True as that may be, I know you were listening in the library. Ballard explained it to your father. Your pair-bond with the black dragon, combined with the Birthright of the queens of old, shows that you're indeed our new queen. That's good enough for us simple folks."

"So, what? Now you steal me away to rule over the treacherous mercenaries?"

"Pretty much, but we have to save your dragon first. Let's just hope you're worth the chaos this is going to cause. If we lose any men over trying to bring back a traitor's daughter, then the dragon got it wrong."

I raised my brows at his words and crossed my arms, anger seeping from me. Seeing my reaction, he stalked over to me, invading my personal space, and looked me up and down.

"I see I've managed to offend you, fair lady. Get used to it because your life as a proper young noble is over. Welcome to the clan. I hope you adjust fast enough to survive because we leave the weak ones in the dust." With that, he grabbed hold of my dressing gown and ripped it off me.

I shrieked and flinched away from him, waiting for the next blow to land on me. When nothing else happened, I peeked out from behind my hands to see Cole no longer standing in front of me. I turned to find him out on the balcony tying my gown and sheets together to make a rope.

"We're going to climb down from the balcony, and that coat would have gotten in the way. Tie your dress and hurry up or I'll toss your royal ass over," he said as he worked, not looking at me.

"You wouldn't dare!"

"Try me, little mouse. I have a job to do, and you're not going to stop me."

I shook myself from my fear of being hit and straightened my shoulders. I couldn't believe I showed Cole I was afraid of him.

"All right. Everything's ready," Cole announced. "I'll climb down first, and you follow after me. The rope doesn't make it all the way to the ground, but it's just a short fall. I think you'll manage."

I walked to the edge and looked over. I'd never really thought it was that far up, but I did now. I watched as Cole simply slid down the makeshift rope and landed lightly in the courtyard. Now it was my turn.

Taking a few deep breaths, I climbed over the railing and grabbed hold of the sheet, clutching the stone tightly as I tried to wrap my legs around the sheets. When I felt as ready as I could, I let go of the railing and slowly made my way down. Almost to the end, I felt the sheets loosen, and I looked up just in time to see the knot around the railing untie. I came crashing down, landing in a heap, the sheet rope scattering around me. I groaned as I sat up. Slowly, I stood and brushed off the dirt from my clothes, glaring at Cole, who was laughing under his breath, holding his stomach as he tried to keep from bursting into full-blown guffaws.

"Well, I guess we'll have to work on that," Cole said, trying to pull himself together.

SIX

THE PLAN

"**S**low down, I don't have any shoes on, and I'm in my night-gown," I whined, crossing my arms to cover my breasts and stepping on yet another stone.

"Consider this a crash course into your new reality, little mouse. It's called making the best out of what you have," Cole shot back over his shoulder.

"I have a name, you know."

"Yeah, and when you stop squealing like a mouse, I'll use it."

Stopping in the middle of the road, I flopped to the ground to dig out the gravel from my feet, letting out a frustrated scream. "I'm not taking one more step like this. I'm not some prisoner you can drag around as you please in the middle of the night. You keep telling me I'm going to be a queen, but you treat me like a criminal."

Cole stomped over to me, his eyes flashing with his anger, hands balled into fists, but he didn't move toward me. Turning, he let out a whistle that sounded like a bird call and waited. A few moments later, three hooded men seemed to materialize out of the woods like mist.

I quickly jumped to my feet and hid behind Cole's body, unnerved by their sudden appearance. Why I thought Cole would protect me if something bad went down was beyond me, but it was all I could think to do. Thankfully, we had nothing to fear from these men because I wasn't sure I was ready to see where his loyalties were regarding my safety.

"I see you've managed to safely bring the queen's heir out of the manor. Nice to see that even an asshole like you can do something so simple without screwing it up." One of the men scoffed at Cole.

"I get the feeling you're jealous, Richard. Are you butthurt because I was chosen over you to get her out safely?" Cole asked.

The young man tossed back his hood, revealing his proud features and glaring bright blue eyes.

"Some of us have to earn our right to wear that symbol you have around your neck. Unlike others, who are simply born within the right family," Richard snarled, pointing at the necklace I noticed Cole wore. It was a simple black metal medallion with a blooming rose and a dragon flying across it, but its meaning was lost on me.

"You can keep bitching if it helps you sleep at night, but we all know why you still haven't been given yours," Cole said, his body tense and ready to act. "Where are the horses? We need to get *Lady* Cassarah to the meeting spot, or this whole thing will fall apart. Then whose fuck-up will that be?"

"Why is she only in a nightgown? Didn't you let the poor woman get dressed before you dragged her through the woods? She's going to be your queen, and you show her such disrespect?" Richard asked, shocked to see what I was wearing.

"Give her your own damn cloak if you're worried about it," Cole spat, brushing past Richard into the woods, the other two men following him.

Richard walked over to me, taking off his cloak and wrapping it around me. "There, that should be better. And a bit warmer on this chilly night."

Cole and the others returned with horses, Richard and the other two swiftly mounting theirs while Cole double-checked the saddle on his mount. It seemed as if he was trying to collect himself. Apparently, something Richard said seemed to have set him off.

"Do I have a horse to ride?" I asked, breaking the strained silence.

"You'll ride behind me. It'll be faster since we know where we're going," Cole said.

I was a little taken aback by this statement. It was improper for a young woman to be that close to a man who wasn't her husband. I cleared my throat to say so, but before I could get the words out, he'd mounted his horse and held out his hand to me. I looked at it dumbly, unsure of the right choice in this situation. I didn't have any training on how to deal with mercenaries or their customs.

"We don't have all night, little mouse. You can sit atop the horse properly, or I can sling you over like a sack of potatoes. Your choice," Cole said, sighing deeply, obviously tired of dealing with me.

Knowing I didn't have any other choice, I grasped his hand tightly and was slung up behind him. When I settled myself as comfortably as I could behind the saddle, I looked for a place to hold onto something—anything that wasn't him. Before I could figure that out, Cole kicked his horse into motion, forcing me to cling to him or fall off.

Once balanced, I loosened my hold on him and found my rhythm with the horse's movements. My cheeks flamed red with embarrassment as my chest pressed to his back, and I felt Cole's hard abs under my hands. I tried to hold on without feeling like I was groping him, but I wasn't sure I succeeded.

For some odd reason, his citrus and pine scent set me at ease. I wanted to let my cheek rest against his strong back, but I knew he would not be pleased with me touching him more than necessary. Unfortunately, he was the only somewhat familiar thing around me, and it was apparently playing tricks on my mind. I knew he didn't like me, so I shouldn't let myself be drawn to him.

It didn't take us long to get to the Royal City limits since cutting through the woods was a more direct route than taking the main road. Cole and the others reined in their horses and dismounted quickly, and I followed suit as fast as I could, nearly landing on the ground again. I noticed there were ten other horses that'd been left in the woods along with our four. These must belong to Ballard and the others, which meant I was close to getting some answers about what was going on.

Apparently, though, I was mistaken about being close to our destination. It seemed we still had some walking to do.

"Do you really expect me to keep walking barefoot in the dark?" I asked Cole, peering out from under the large hood of Richard's cloak.

"Yes. Now be quiet. We can't risk anyone in the city alerting the captain of the King's Guard we're here," he grumbled.

"So it would be bad for me to start screaming that I've been kidnapped, right?"

Cole stopped and looked back at me as if he wanted to strangle me. "That would be a very bad idea, little mouse. If you're feeling such urges, let me warn you that I will gladly gag you to prevent events like that from happening."

"No need to go to such drastic measures. If someone would simply carry me so I don't have to keep walking and getting stabbed in the foot, I wouldn't feel the need to alert anyone to my plight."

"Goddamn fucking prissy maidens. How the hell did I get stuck with this shit job," Cole muttered as he kneeled in front of me. "Hop on and be quick about it."

Not wanting him to change his mind, I scrambled onto his back, wrapping my arms around his neck. He tucked his arms around my legs as he stood, keeping me from sliding off. I grinned from under my hood, pleased I had finally won an argument. Thankfully, we moved much faster now that I wasn't slowing them down.

When we reached the outer edge of the city, Richard led us into a small, nondescript alehouse that reeked of stale ale and unwashed men. Cole dropped me on my feet and headed up a steep staircase into an attic room.

"You're here at last! You boys made good time. Did you bring her with you, Cole?" Ballard asked from where he sat at a low table.

Cole's answer to his grandfather's question was to simply pull back the hood of my cloak, revealing my face to the rest of the room.

"Come, sit. You've had a busy night," Ballard said as he stood and pulled out a chair for me.

I smiled at him as I gratefully took my seat. At least someone in this group knew how to treat a proper lady. I looked down at the table to see it covered in various maps of the city and the castle. Surprised and immediately curious, I leaned in to get a closer look at the maps of the castle. They were so detailed they had to have been made by someone who had spent a significant amount of time there.

"What do you need with a map of the castle?" I asked no one in general.

The room was silent for a moment, causing me to look up at Ballard.

"Didn't Cole explain everything to you?" he asked, frowning. The blank look on my face must have answered that question for him.

"Tomorrow, with your help, we are planning on saving your dragon and getting you both out of Royal City. Once we get you back to the clan lands, then you will be crowned our queen."

"Don't let her fool you, Granddad. She was in the library when we were talking to her father. She knows more than she's letting on," Cole said, scowling at me.

"It seems that mercenary blood runs strong in you, no matter how hard your family tried to smother it out of you," Ballard said with a grin.

Seeing that playing dumb wasn't going to get Cole in trouble or gain me more information, I went back over the facts I had in front of me. "So how do you plan on getting into the castle? From what I can tell, we have limited options, and none seem ideal for sneaking in unnoticed."

With that question, all eyes in the room were on me. Some held surprise while others held mistrust at my conclusion. They didn't know it was one of the games my father and I played when we both got bored studying past wars. Instead of just reading about our history, we would get out maps and relive the battle as if we were both commanding officers planning our next move. In some cases, we found that a battle could have been won if they'd looked harder at what they were dealing with.

Ballard cleared his throat and took a large gulp of his ale before he answered me. "I agree with you. There are not many ways to get in and out of the castle. As you saw, most places will get us spotted. Although I think if we take a different approach, it might be easier than we thought."

"What do you mean?" I asked.

"We don't need to sneak into the castle. We can just walk in," Ballard said, smiling down at me.

My mind raced to catch up to what he was saying, then under-standing finally hit. I was a member of the court as well as pair-bonded to a dragon, which gave me the right to enter the palace whenever I wanted. I'd been thinking about this the wrong way—there was no need for me to sneak into the castle and steal what was already mine.

"I think she gets it, lads." Ballard chuckled.

"There is one small problem. I can't just walk into the palace dressed like this and on foot. It's just simply not done. There is a proper protocol I have to go through, not to mention that the queen might want to see me," I said as I ran through the scenario in my mind.

"Don't you think we've thought of that already? Our last member should be joining us in the morning once they finish their end of the plan," Ballard answered, his eyes shining with mischief. "For now, we will sleep. Especially you. We need you bright-eyed and clear-headed for this whole thing to go off without a hitch."

I looked around the room again, not seeing any door that might lead to another bedroom. Where did they assume I was going to sleep? Did they have other rooms in the inn for use? Hopefully, they would be nicer than this room—there was no telling what rodents might be sharing the same space as us right now.

"We curtained off this area here for you to sleep. I know it's not what you're used to, but we did the best we could. If Lord Everett gets tipped off that we're here, then the whole plan is going to fall apart," Ballard said as he walked over to the far corner of the room and pulled back a blanket they'd tacked up.

I stood, clutching my cloak around me as I examined the accom-modations they'd pulled together. The cot was stuffed with straw, and the pillow looked like a herd of horses had trampled on it, but at least the blanket seemed thick and warm.

"I'm to sleep here?" I gulped.

"What's that? Do I hear a little mouse squeaking again?" Cole whispered right behind me, scaring an actual squeak out of me.

Cole laughed as he walked away, immensely pleased with himself. Glaring at his back, I stomped behind the blanket and sat on the straw mattress in the soft glow the worn barrier let in. Wrapping myself fully in the cloak so no part of me touched the pallet, I laid down and pulled the wool blanket over me, listening to the men's voices on the other side as they finalized the plans for tomorrow.

Was I crazy to trust these people? Did I have any choice? There was no way that I could save Vasin on my own. If I couldn't do what it took to save him, then it was like giving up my own life.

Could a plan this simple truly work?

Finally, I drifted off to sleep going through different scenarios of how things could go wrong tomorrow.

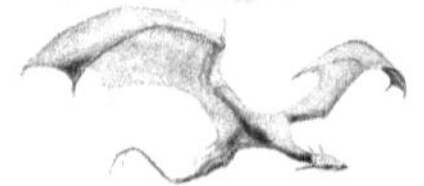

"Rise and shine, lazy bones. You have a dragon to save, and it's the middle of the afternoon." Becka's voice, followed by the aggressive shaking of my shoulder, woke me from my fitful night's sleep.

Seeing Becka kneeling next to me made me think that everything from last night might have been a dream until I saw where I was. Sitting up, my mind was in a frenzy trying to figure out how she was connected to all this. I'd never been so surprised in my life. What in the world was she doing *here*?

"You can't get rid of me that easily, Cassarah." Becka grinned, her bright blue eyes crinkling.

I stood up from my pallet and threw my arms around her. I was so glad to have a friendly face in all of this that it didn't matter how she got here. She hugged me back just as tightly, and I could feel her relief in my response to her presence. I stepped back from her and looked her up and down as if I had missed something in all the years I'd known her.

"How are you here? What about my parents? Won't they think it's strange we're both missing?" I couldn't get the questions out fast enough.

"My family is part of the Raven Rose clan, and we were initially sent to keep an eye on your family. They needed to make sure your family wouldn't be a threat to us. When my parents decided your father wouldn't sell us out, they left, but I stayed behind to watch over you. I couldn't abandon you with a mother like that... I wouldn't have been able to live with myself," Becka answered. "I would have followed you and Cole, but my job was to make sure your family knew we'd taken you, and if they said a word about it to anyone, we would ruin them in the eyes of the court."

"There is plenty of time to talk later, Becka. We need to get her ready so we can leave on time," Ballard said, interrupting our reunion.

"Yes, of course. If you'll all leave the room, I will knock when it's safe to come back in," Becka instructed.

They'd supplied a tarnished mirror and a small three-legged stool. I looked at Becka, raising an eyebrow in distaste. She just smiled and started to pull clothing out of a canvas sack.

"Put these leggings on. It will be easier for you to get away in those if something goes wrong."

I did as Becka directed, and when I'd slipped the floor-length chemise on, she took a knife and cut the seams on either side. "This will make it easier for you to ride astride a horse if need be."

I nodded, trusting her judgment, knowing she would keep me safe any way she could. Next came a simple dress made of dark emerald-green velvet. She finished by wrapping a silver chain belt around my waist twice and clasping it, letting the extra drape down the front.

"I think you should wear boots. Slippers won't do you any good if you have to get away quickly. Besides, no one will look at your feet since your face and chest are distracting enough." Becka winked as she braided my hair loosely to the side.

I laughed and smacked Becka for her crude joke. It was fun to see her free to be herself, not having to worry about anyone hearing us or finding out and being punished.

"That should do it! I would say you are more than presentable to enter the palace," she said with a proud smile.

I glanced into the tarnished mirror and took a deep breath. Now I just had to figure out how to act normal while at court.

Becka let the men back into the attic, and I was surprised to see that six of them had changed into livery with my family crest. Ballard had truly thought of everything to be able to pull this off on such short notice.

"So, do we look presentable enough to be your escorts?" Ballard asked.

He was dressed in the same manner as a male attendant, which was the proper custom when a single lady went to visit another home. I smiled and gave Ballard one of my best curtsies, showing my approval. Scanning the men, I looked to see if Cole would be coming with us to the palace or remain outside in case we needed extra help. I found him hiding in the corner, looking out the small window wearing a frown, dressed in my family's colors.

"Cassarah, I'll meet you back on clan lands once I make sure your parents keep their mouths shut after you and Vasin take off," Becka said, hugging me goodbye.

"Shall we go? Your carriage is waiting out back for you," Ballard said as he held his arm out for me.

I grasped his arm lightly, following him down the stairs and out the back door to be met with a simple two-person buggy. Richard was waiting next to the buggy, ready to assist me into my seat like the good footman he was pretending to be. Ballard walked to the other side and sat opposite me as the others mounted their horses. It must have shown on my face how worried I was because Ballard squeezed my hand in reassurance.

Seeing as we were already in the city, I was surprised at how long it took us to get from the outskirts to the castle. Now that it was fall, the days were getting shorter, and I knew Ballard was worried about running out of daylight.

A guard from the front gate walked up to the buggy and bowed. "May I inquire as to the reason for your visit to the palace?"

"This is Lady Cassarah, pair-bond to the black dragon," Ballard responded.

The guard looked at me in surprise, then bowed to me once again and waved for the gates to be opened. "Welcome back to the palace, Lady Cassarah."

Once through the gates, Ballard murmured, "See, I told you it would be easy to get in. Getting out will be tricky since a dragon is not a small thing to hide."

Taking a few deep breaths, I tried to calm myself. All I had to do now was get to the roost. Then I remembered something about that—there were only two ways to get there. Through the palace like I'd gone the first time was the fastest, and the other was to travel through the large garden maze. It was set up that way so if the city was attacked, the roost would be the last place they could get to.

I gulped as I tried to remember how I'd gotten there from the main entrance. There had been so many stops along the way. Once I was in the right hallway, I'm sure I could remember the way. I just had to look for things I recognized.

"Shall we go in?" Ballard asked at my elbow.

"Let's do this." Squaring my shoulders and lifting my skirt, I made my way up to the palace entrance.

SEVEN

DRAGON RESCUE

As Ballard and I approached the palace's massive double doors, they creaked open, showing an elderly gentleman dressed in a bright red jacket, marking him as palace staff. He bowed to me, then signaled for us to follow him without a single word spoken. For some reason, that made me feel nervous, and I feared we'd already been discovered and were being taken somewhere to be punished. Sensing my emotions, Ballard gently squeezed my arm, reminding me I wasn't alone.

The gentleman ushered us into a sitting room with a warm, cheerful fire to ward off the chill the stone castle seemed to have. "Please wait here for a moment. The queen is unable to greet you, but one of her attendants is being sent along with her greeting."

Upon hearing that the queen was busy, a weight lifted off my shoulders. I didn't think I could lie to Queen Mary's face since she'd been so kind to me. I took a deep breath and relaxed into the armchair, feeling we might be able to really pull this thing off. Once we finished this meeting, we would be able to walk freely through the palace and complete our mission. A sharp knock sounded on the door, surprising me out of my thoughts. I stood ready to greet the person, but when they didn't walk through the door right away, I was unsure of what to do.

"You may enter," Ballard called.

The door opened, and a handsome man walked through, bowing to me. "Greetings, Lady Cassarah. I regret to inform you that Queen Mary cannot come and greet you properly. She has urgent matters to attend to, so she sent her humble servant instead."

I was so taken aback by the depth of this man's voice and how it resonated around the room, it took me a moment to remember my manners. I hastily curtsied and replied, "I am honored at the queen's attention. She is very gracious toward a humble subject such as myself."

In response, I received a dashing smile, and his deep blue eyes glinted with humor and mischief. "Forgive me, but I must correct you on that. You are no longer a nobody... you are the woman pair-bonded to the black dragon. That fact alone makes you someone the crown would keep as a close friend, just in case. I would get out of the mindset that you are just another silly palace court lady. You are far more valuable than any of them."

I could feel Ballard tense, pulling me behind him as he seemed to sense—just as I did—realizing this was not just any old palace attendant. He was too familiar with information about me.

"At the fear of sounding rude, may I ask who you are?" I inquired, peering around Ballard while floundering to come up with something better to say to these outlandish remarks.

The man took a better look at Ballard as if seeing him for the first time. His mouth turned down a little at the corners as if displeased.

They seemed to size each other up for a moment before Ballard bowed deeply to the handsome man.

"Your Highness, I apologize. I didn't recognize you... please forgive my rudeness," Ballard said reverently, moving to the side.

"All is forgiven. You were doing your duty in keeping your charge safe," the man said, then turned his attention to me. "Sadly, my game has now been ruined. As your manservant has discovered, I am Crown Prince Gavin of our humble kingdom."

I felt my mouth gape in shock. I was speaking to the man I might have had a chance of marrying. I looked at him with new eyes. His thick, curly, dark blond hair brushed his shoulders and swept gently across his forehead. His bone structure was just like his father's as were the brilliant blue eyes that shone warmly at me. How could I have missed it when it was so plain to see?

"It is an honor to meet you, Your Highness," I answered once I shook off my shock, giving him my best curtsy.

"When I heard you came to the palace, I couldn't help myself. I wanted to meet you. Sadly, I had other business to attend to on the day you were presented at court. I was hoping you wouldn't find out who I was. It's more fun that way, and people are more relaxed. Still, it was worth it. It's not every day that the woman pair-bonded to the black dragon stops by your home." Prince Gavin grinned excitedly, making him seem even more charming.

"I'm afraid not everyone feels the same way you do. I've been trying to keep a low profile, which is why my family sent me abroad for a time. Yet when I heard that Vasin was in danger, I had to come and see him," I said, keeping with the story that my family had been telling people.

"Then let me escort you to the roost so you may see for yourself that your dragon is in perfect health. I'll warn you, though, dragons grow fast. Mother tells me he's grown larger than most his age," Prince Gavin said as he walked toward the door, holding it open for me.

I looked back at Ballard, and he nodded slightly, letting me know we should just follow along. If we had the prince escorting us, we shouldn't have any complications getting to the roost. I followed him silently, not knowing if I should say anything without him asking me a question first. Ballard trailed behind us a few steps to give us the illusion of privacy, not that I felt we needed it.

"How was your stay abroad? I hear it's the first time you've left your family's home," Prince Gavin asked casually.

"It was nice to be able to have some time away and be somewhere new. I didn't get out much, though, with all the tutors my mother sent along with me," I shared, trying to be as truthful as I could.

"Your mother sounds a lot like mine," he said, giving me an understanding smile.

"I doubt that," I grumbled, the disdain for my mother hot on my tongue. Immediately, I blushed, knowing how rude that sounded but decided to carry on. "I've never met another person who could equal my mother's drive. Nothing I do is quite good enough for her. Everything always has to be perfect, no matter the circumstances. As her only child, she has all her hopes pinned on me. It's a lot to deal with at times, especially since she wants me to somehow magically remove my pair-bond with Vasin."

I was not typically so free with my words. I'd learned long ago that anything you said would be used against you at some point in your life. Yet, for some reason, the prince seemed to set me at ease. The more I talked to him, the more comfortable I felt with him.

I glanced over to see what his reaction was to my rant. He just stopped and looked at me with understanding in his eyes. From that one look, I felt he truly understood the pain of having to be forced into something you were never meant to be.

"I am truly sorry to hear that. Your mother should be proud of the fact you have a dragon, no matter the color. It's a great honor. Even if any of the stories are true about the black dragon being evil, she should believe in you to do the right thing," he answered softly, resting his hand lightly on my arm.

I felt as if I'd finally found someone who fully understood what I was going through. I smiled shyly at him and dropped my gaze, feeling that the moment had become much too intimate.

"I'm sure my life is no comparison to the pressures you must be under. Forgive me for complaining, but thank you for listening. That was kind of you," I murmured, unsure of where to direct the conversation from here. I never did learn the art of flirting effortlessly.

"Forgive me, Your Highness, but I do have to have Lady Cassarah home soon. It's getting late in the day," Ballard interrupted, startling us both.

The prince cleared his throat and stepped away from me, letting his hand fall from my arm. "Of course, it's not much farther. Just through the garden and the large gate straight ahead."

"It was a pleasure, Your Highness. Hopefully, we might meet again." I smiled, giving him a curtsy.

"The pleasure is all mine, Lady Cassarah." Prince Gavin bowed, retreating down the hall.

A few moments later, Ballard and I were in the large garden, the roost in view just on the other side of the stone wall.

"Come. We must move quickly. We've already taken much longer than we should have. They plan to attack at dark, but it would be bad if any of the men decided to take matters into their own hands," Ballard said as he guided me through the garden.

We walked as calmly as we could, not wanting anyone to take much notice of us. I could feel my skin vibrating with anticipation at seeing Vasin again. I didn't realize how lost I felt without being able to feel him close by. He had become so much a part of who I was in such a short time. I could only imagine what it would be like now that we were going to be together.

"Easy now, take a deep breath," Ballard instructed. "You feel like a nervous colt."

I looked up at him, surprised. I'd forgotten for a moment that I wasn't alone on this journey. Nodding, I took a few deep, calming breaths and tried to get my nerves under control. It was all I could do to keep from running the last few steps to the large double doors that blocked me from my dragon.

"Halt!" a voice called out. "This area is off limits to all those who are not pair-bonded."

I hadn't noticed there were two guards stationed outside the entrance to the roost. I didn't remembered there being any the last time I'd been here. *Could they have been placed here to keep Vasin safe from the recent attacks?*

"This is Lady Cassarah, pair-bonded to the black dragon, Vasin," Ballard announced to the guards.

One of the guards stepped forward with a torch in the fading sunlight to get a better look at my face. The bright light of the torch blinded me for a moment before I recognized he was one of Lord Everett's guards. I gasped, and the next moment, I was knocked over by Ballard as he blocked a dagger that had been meant for me.

"Run! Get to the roost and get Vasin out of there!" Ballard called out.

Dazed, it took a moment before what he'd said made sense. When it registered, I scrambled to my feet and took off, ignoring the fact I'd almost been stabbed. The entrance was in sight, but as I got closer, two other guards stepped out of the lengthening shadows and blocked my way, swords drawn.

"By orders of the captain of the King's Guard, Lord Everett, we cannot let you pass," one of them called out as he advanced on me.

Panic rose in my chest, making it hard to think clearly. I looked around wildly, trying to come up with some idea on how to proceed. I'd been taught many useful things in my life, but dealing with this kind of situation was not one of them. Moments before I realized a guard was going to strike me down with a sword, a shadow descended upon him, smashing him into the ground. It was then that I noticed the other guard was bleeding out on the ground, and my way was clear. Even then, I still couldn't seem to compel myself to move from where I was standing. Fear had frozen my body. Then I was filled with a warm sensation that seemed to melt the bonds that my fear had created.

"*Cass, you have returned to me.*" Vasin's voice suddenly echoed in my head.

That was all it took for me to take off running headlong toward the doors, leaping over the fallen body of one of the guards. Once I reached the door, I grabbed the large metal ring and, with all my strength, tried to pull it open. Despite my efforts, the door wouldn't budge.

"Vasin, help me!" I cried in desperation, tears streaming down my face as fear tried to choke me.

How could I have been chosen by a dragon to be its pair-bond? I was no one special. I didn't have any useful skills. I wasn't even able to save my other half when he was in danger.

"*I am here for you. Just open up to me, and I will give you the strength you need.*" Vasin's soothing voice surrounded me and calmed my emotions.

"How do I do that?" I yelled internally, desperately trying to under-stand what he was talking about.

Then I remembered the times I'd tried to connect with him when I was at home. We'd been too far apart for it to work, but now he was only a few feet away. I took a few steps back, took a few deep breaths, and closed my eyes, shutting out the sounds of the fighting behind me. I centered myself until I could feel that piece of me that connected to Vasin and grasped it. The moment I held it, I was filled with a warm, rich sensation that made me feel like I was whole for the first time in my life. I let that sensation flow over me, and I felt Vasin and I were truly one being. I now knew what I had to do and would succeed because I wasn't alone anymore.

Opening my eyes, it took a moment for me to focus since I was sharing my sight with Vasin. Seeing the world through his eyes was a bit overwhelming.

"Focus on the task at hand," Vasin scolded. *"You must learn balance when handling our combined power."*

I shook my head and tried to ignore all the information I had at my fingertips and just focus on getting into the roost. I inhaled deeply, raising my arms to aim the bow that had materialized in my hands. I held my breath for a second as I aimed at the door and smoothly let out that breath as I let the arrow fly. The arrow flew straight and true, burrowing itself deep into the wooden doors. The world seemed to pause for a second before the doors burst, shattering into thousands of pieces with a loud explosion, knocking me to the ground. Feeling disoriented with Vasin's sudden absence from my thoughts, I decided to lay there for a moment and gather myself before I even tried to stand.

"If I had known that you would be more trouble than your dragon, then I would've made sure to kill you first," a voice snarled from the darkness behind me.

I sat up but quickly fell back to the ground, drained and too dizzy to go anywhere. I shut my eyes tightly, hoping that magically, Lord Everett wouldn't be standing there and would just disappear. My eyes flew open when cool steel touched my throat, bringing me eye to eye with Lord Everett's hard gaze. There was nothing but hatred in that look, and it was all directed at me.

"The battle is in full swing, and there's no one to save you this time," he gloated, pleased by my fear. "I've been waiting for the day I could rid the world of scum like Ballard's clan. Thank you for bringing them here to me. Now when I tell the queen they attacked the castle and killed you in the process, I'll have the approval I need to hunt down the others. They have no clue what the black dragon really means. I, however, haven't forgotten our history. There is no way I'll let those mercenary scum have their little queen and her dragon so they can kill us all in our beds."

As he raised his sword, I felt his tremendous anger and hatred hurtling toward me. Then the sound of heavy wing beats surrounded us, and I curled up into a little ball as Vasin snatched Lord Everett into the air. I could hear him yelling and cursing Vasin as he was tossed into the moat outside the palace wall with a loud splash.

I sat up slowly, drained of energy and terrified. The wind whipped around me, sending dust and leaves scattering in all directions. I covered my face with my arms, trying to keep the worst of it out of my eyes. When the wind died down, I peered over my arms and was met with bright amber eyes. Without thinking, I grabbed Vasin's face and hugged it tightly, rubbing my cheek against his soft, scaled face. In response, I could hear him humming, the sound vibrating against my cheek and through my body.

"You're safe! I was so worried you'd get hurt before I could get to you," I gushed when I finally let him go.

"*I AM FINE, MY DEAR CASS, BUT I PUT YOU AT RISK WITH NO ONE TO PROTECT YOU.*"

"What are you talking about? You came to my rescue. I owe you my life." I frowned, not understanding why he was so upset.

"*I SHOULD HAVE WARNED YOU THAT YOU WOULD BE DRAINED OF ENERGY AFTER HARMONIZING. MY JOB IS TO KEEP YOU SAFE, NOT THE OTHER WAY AROUND,*" he said, letting out a low rumble at something I couldn't see.

Finally, getting a good look at him, I realized how large he'd grown while I was away. His body was about the size of a draft horse, and his tail trailed out even farther behind him. His wings were tucked away, but the sheer size of them told you how wide they would be if unfurled. His black scales glinted in the torchlight, making him look like living liquid metal.

"Cassarah!" Cole's worried voice called out of the darkness. "Get out of there… it's a trap!" He grunted like he'd gotten hit. "They knew we were coming! *Go!*"

"Where are we supposed to go?" I cried out.

I trembled against Vasin, terrified at the thought I had no idea what to do. A proper lady didn't have to fear for her life—she was safe at home with her husband. Now here I was, alone in the dark with no clue how to proceed.

"*YOU'RE NOT ALONE, CASS,*" Vasin said, swinging his head around to face me. "*Climb onto my back. We'll go to the mountains. It will be safe there.*"

I nodded my head and crawled onto his back. Using his bent leg as a step, I found a comfortable place at the base of his neck and rested my feet on his shoulders to keep balance. When Vasin expanded his wings and gave a great heave that sent us springing into the air, I clutched his neck, fearing I would fall to my death from such a great height.

"*I WILL NOT DROP YOU. YOU WILL ALWAYS BE SAFE WITH ME.*"

The air was chilly as the night wind buffeted my face and pulled at my skirts. I hunkered down as close as I could to Vasin's body, but that didn't help much since his scales were cool to the touch. I would have to find a way to make a barrier between his scales and my skin the next time we flew. Even though it was a cold ride, it was still the most exhilarating experience of my life. Listening to the steady beat of his massive wings and watching the ground below pass by lit only by the moon's cool glow was magical.

After some time, Vasin started to descend into a clearing deep in the woods, far away from the castle. The landing was soft and graceful for a beast of his size. I swiftly slid off his shoulder, only to fall in a heap on the ground. Clearly, I wasn't nearly as agile.

"*WE WILL SPEND THE NIGHT HERE. YOU NEED TO REST,*" Vasin said, nuzzling my cheek with his nose.

"Here, out in the *woods*?" I questioned, wringing my hands as I looked around. "What about wolves or bears? They could come and attack us out in the open."

"*CASS, WHO DO YOU THINK IS SCARIER? ME OR THE WOOD-LAND CREATURES?*"

Pouting, I knew he was right, but I still didn't love the idea of having to sleep outside with all the bugs.

"*COME. I MADE YOU A SOFT BED OF LEAVES. I WILL KEEP YOU WARM AND SAFE. YOU HAVE NOTHING TO FEAR WHILE I AM WATCHING OVER YOU.*"

Walking over to him, I sighed before settling into the bed he'd made. Vasin tucked me in close to his chest, where I felt a warmth radiating from him. Miraculously, I was so tired that the last thing I remembered was Vasin snuffling my hair and resting his elegant head nearby with a contented croon.

EIGHT

ROUGHING IT

When I awoke, I was alone in the clearing of tall grass sur-rounding me. The world around me was hazy, like a mist hung in the air. I rubbed my eyes, trying to see if my vision was the problem, but it didn't change anything. Since I'd never been away from home, I wasn't sure if this was normal for the mountains. I looked around, trying to find where Vasin had wandered off to. He should be easy to find since he didn't blend in with the rich green foliage, but I couldn't see him anywhere. Unsure of what to do, I decided to go look for him. I grunted slightly as I stood, feeling stiff and sore, which was to be expected after riding a dragon and sleeping on the ground.

A well-worn deer path ran near where I stood, so I followed it aim-lessly, not knowing where else to go. I paused and tried reaching out to him mentally through our connection, but I couldn't feel him at all. The place in my chest I'd grown accustomed to being a hollow ache was now empty. Something had to be wrong.

When I tried again, a flash of anguish pulsed through my body, causing me to fall to my knees and gasp. It felt like my soul was being torn apart, and nothing in this world would fix it. What had once filled that space in my heart was gone, ripped away from me, never to return. I let out a sob, clutching my chest, but rose to my feet. Something told me I needed to keep moving, that it wasn't safe to stay here. I turned toward the mountains, knowing it was the only chance I had to survive.

Feeling utterly numb, just putting one foot in front of the other, something caused me to pause. Listening carefully, I heard a twig snap off to the right. I swiveled my head, closed my eyes, and let the forest speak to me. How I knew to do this was beyond me, but I trusted my instincts.

In the silence, I heard more twigs snapping, closer this time. I was being followed. I was in danger, and if I didn't get away, I would die. Dashing through the trees, I didn't question the need to flee.

Moments later, breaking out of the forest onto a well-used dirt road, I was face-to-face with Lord Everett and his army. I stood stunned in the middle of the road, paralyzed, taking in the sight before me.

Wait!

That man wasn't Lord Everett. It was a different man altogether, dressed in the royal guard colors.

"You didn't think you could get away from me that easily, did you?" he sneered, drawing his sword from its sheath. "Your men perished trying to give you a chance to get away, but it wasn't enough. You should know, though, they died still professing their love for their whore of a queen."

His words made no sense to me, but the pain they brought to my heart was almost as intense as the void in my soul.

I might not know who he was, but I knew he was going to kill me.

Turning on my heel, I took off running down the road as fast as I could. I knew I couldn't outrun him on horseback, so I looked for the perfect place to duck back into the forest. As I ran, the trees seemed to thin and become sparser, and the ground turned rocky. I must be close to the mountain's foothills. The sound of hoofbeats drove me on. I tried to climb up a rocky ledge and out of sight before they gained on me.

"Don't lose her. We need to bring back her head to the king and queen," the crazy man called out.

I stumbled as my foothold came loose, and rocks cascaded down the hill below me. I scrambled to keep ahead of the shifting rocks, but the skirt of my dress kept getting snagged, slowing me down.

I had to get away. I couldn't let them use me to control Vasin. Why hadn't I asked Father to teach me anything I could use as self-defense? At the moment, I was as weak as a baby, and there was nothing I could do but run to stay alive.

"There she is! She's climbing the ledge. Get her down before she gets away!" bellowed a voice from below me.

Unable to find a way to climb any farther, I just clung to the rock ledge, praying that someone would save me.

Then a thought crossed my mind—I didn't have anything else to live for. My men were killed, my dragon slaughtered before my eyes, so what was left for me? Even if I made it back to my people, I would be a hollow excuse for a queen.

They were wrong about dying when your dragon is killed. You don't die right away. It happens slowly, painfully, and the feeling of being half a person tortured you to finally end it yourself. If I were going to die, then let this last act of being their queen count for something. I couldn't protect the men I loved or my soul in dragon form, but I could save the future of my people.

Taking one last breath, I shoved off the ledge as hard as I could, pulling my last dagger out of its spot on my lower back. I aimed true, falling right into the thick of the reaching hands below, vowing to take down as many of them as I could. The air rushed past me, warm and gentle, soothing my worries and letting me know I'd made the right *decision. I would give my own life to save those of my people and their families, even if they never knew what truly happened. My child would grow up without her mother or her fathers, but I was going to keep her safe. It was my calling, my destiny, and I was doing something meaningful with my life.*

Then the world went still, black, and silent. A glowing woman's face shone before my eyes and then was gone before I could make out her features.

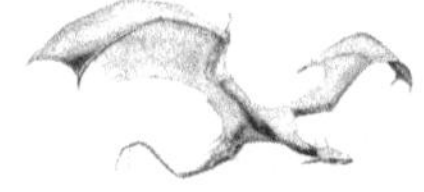

"Cassarah, come back to me," Vasin said, waking me from the darkness.

I gasped, lurching forward, my open eyes gazing into a large golden gaze filled with worry. I frowned when I saw him, not understanding what he was doing here or how I was still alive.

Then I noticed the sun was just cresting over the treetops, flooding the meadow with soft light. *Why was I back here?* I'd been half a day's walk toward the mountains, last I remembered.

"What just happened? You were crying and shaking a moment ago, then suddenly you stopped breathing," Vasin said, pulling me out of my memories.

"That was all a dream? No, there's no way it could've been just a dream. It was so real," I said, wiping away the tears still on my cheeks.

Vasin watched me carefully, not sure what to do with me. Then he blinked slowly and settled his head in the grass near my side. "Tell me. I might be able to help you understand it."

"I woke up, just like this, but you were gone. I went to look for you, but when I couldn't find you, I headed for the mountains. On my way, I was caught by the King's Guard and his men. He said something about killing my men and that I was next.

"I started running, but I wasn't fast enough and couldn't get away, so I began to climb up the mountainside. When I couldn't climb any farther, I decided it was better to die than to live without my men and dragon."

I could feel my heart racing as I relived the whole event.

"How can you be right here? I thought I lost you. The pain of you being torn away from me hurt so badly. Never have I felt a dream so real." I started to hyperventilate, once again experiencing the pain of emotions I knew deep down weren't my own. "How could I know with absolute certainty that because you died, I would too from grief? Vasin, I don't think it was a dream. I think it was a memory. There is no way I could imagine the excruciating pain of losing you."

Vasin nuzzled his nose into my neck, trying to comfort me. I turned and grasped his head and let fresh tears fall, tears that the woman in my dream never shed. "My heart shattered thinking about five men I loved almost as much as you. Men who gave their lives to save me. I knew the fastest way for me to get back to them and be free of my pain was to die. The final tipping point was the desperate need to protect something I've never known before."

"WHAT DID YOU WANT TO PROTECT SO BADLY THAT YOU WOULD KILL YOURSELF?"

"My daughter and the people she would rule now that I was gone. I knew I was never going to see any of them again, but I was their queen, and if that was my only chance to do something, I was going to do all I could for their future." I paused, thinking about that last thought. "I don't think I've ever felt that strongly about something."

"Then you should be thankful for this dream. It showed you something important you needed to understand and learn about yourself."

"It did show me the power that one woman had in her love for her people. I am a poor choice for a mercenary queen, but getting the chance to learn to love like that is worth a try," I said calmly, feeling like something in my soul settled at this realization.

"Then I suggest that we start looking for them so you can begin your journey."

I looked up at him and smiled. It was nice to have someone to talk to about things that were bothering me. I knew without a doubt he would be there for me.

We were no longer just a woman and her dragon. Ever since we harmonized, I'd felt the change. We'd become one being—heart, mind, and soul. Lumbering to his feet, Vasin stretched a little before unfurling his magnificent wings, letting me know he was ready to take off.

This time when I made my way onto his back, I could see where I was going, unlike last night. The morning sun had warmed up his cool, scaled flesh, so it wasn't as chilly to sit on. Resting my feet on his shoulders, I rubbed my hand along his neck, letting him know I was ready.

Using only his powerful wings, he took off. It was even more impressive in the sun's rays than it had been by moonlight. The sunlight glittered off his scales, creating a look of deadly beauty as we soared through the skies. Vasin took his time, languidly gliding along the air currents, reveling in the freedom of flight. Feeling more relaxed, I gazed wide-eyed at the amazing sights below.

Shimmering rivers journeyed through vast green forests, only to tumble off the high mountain peaks. Vasin followed one such river, weaving our way through the mountains' narrow canyons until we reached a large reservoir. It was filled by the outside river as well as a few smaller streams trickling from the melting snow. The water was clear enough to see fish darting in all directions beneath the surface.

I had the feeling that living in the mountains wouldn't be as bad as I'd originally thought. Vasin and I explored a few other places before we headed to search the foothills for the others. I had no idea what to expect once we found them. We hadn't been prepared for an all-out battle, and I was hoping we hadn't lost anyone because of it. I would forever feel the guilt if someone died because I could not protect myself.

"THEY WON'T SEE IT THAT WAY, CASS. IT'S THEIR JOB TO KEEP YOU SAFE SO YOU CAN HAVE A CHANCE TO SAVE THEM."

"I know you're probably right, but the only reason they were there was because I couldn't do anything without their help," I said, resting my head against his neck. "I couldn't even escape my own house without Cole forcing me."

"THEN THE ONLY WAY TO REPAY THEM IS TO BECOME SOME-ONE THEY CAN RELY ON TO PROTECT THEM."

I nodded, taking his wisdom to heart. I had a lot of work ahead of me to even begin becoming that person. I cringed at the thought of what Cole would think of my plan. He would probably laugh his head off. To him, ruling a group of mercenaries with love and determination would sound so naïve, but I had seen firsthand it could be done.

No matter. I was going to prove to him and his smug face that I could be just as skilled as him.

"I FOUND THEM," Vasin announced as he began his descent onto a rock-covered clearing.

I couldn't see anything when I looked down, but I'd learned from experience those men could hide very well in plain sight. Vasin landed as smoothly as he could with the unsteady ground he descended upon. I gripped tightly to his neck as the ground shifted slightly, sending us pitching forward down the slope before he could counter it with a strong backstroke of his wings.

"Are you all right? I didn't realize how slippery these rocks would be," Vasin apologized.

"I'm fine. And how would you know? It's your first time out of the roost."

"All dragons have the ability to access all the knowledge of past dragons to learn from their experiences."

I was surprised at this news, wondering what it would be like to have the ability to access all of my ancestors' wisdom. I wondered if having someone who could show me the right path would make life easier.

"Lady Cassarah, are you all right?" I heard Ballard's voice call out, bringing me back to the matters at hand.

I looked over at him and gasped, seeing a bandage covering his left eye. "I should be asking if you're all right."

"It's nothing... looks worse than it is. I'll be fine in a few days," he responded, shaking off my comment.

I looked over at Cole, who was standing next to him. He looked unharmed, but he had a grim expression in response to what his grandfather said. Seeing that look, I had a feeling his wound was worse than he was letting on.

I frowned as I slid off Vasin's back and stumbled as the rocks shifted under my feet. Catching my balance, I noticed Cole had taken a step forward as if he was going to catch me. This action seemed to have caught him by surprise too, if his deepening frown was any indication. He glanced at me, and then when he saw I was fine, stepped back beside his grandfather, not looking at me.

"How are the others?" I asked, ending the awkward silence.

"All are accounted for. Some are wounded but nothing life-threatening. All in all, it was a victory for us, but that's all thanks to your dragon. If he hadn't dropped the mastermind into the moat, then we would've had a hell of a time," Ballard informed me, smiling at Vasin.

"TELL HIM THAT I AM GLAD TO HAVE BEEN OF HELP," Vasin said, lowering his head to my level.

"Vasin said he was more than happy to help," I shared, smiling over at Vasin.

"I hate to cut this meeting short, but we should get deeper into the foothills before it gets dark," Cole interjected.

"Quite right. No one followed us, but best we get out of the open just to make sure," Ballard said. "I think it would be safest for you to fly when you can. It's harder to harm someone in the air."

"I will follow your lead without question," I assured him.

Cole started coughing loudly as he walked away, trying to muffle his words. "Let's see how long that lasts."

I scowled at this retreating back, not understanding why he didn't like me. He didn't even know enough about me not to like me.

"There is a large reservoir deep in the foothills. That's where we're going to spend the night. Do you think you can find it?" Ballard asked Vasin.

Vasin answered with an acknowledging croon and bobbed his head slightly.

"Good. Then we'll meet you there." With that, he turned and walked back behind a large boulder, disappearing from sight.

It didn't take long for all the men to mount up and head off into the foothills. It turned out the reservoir they were talking about was the one we'd seen earlier. We beat the others getting there, but I was happy about it as I made my way to the water's edge.

"Finally, I can attempt to wash up. I feel like I have a week's worth of grime all over my body," I grumbled.

It was icy but refreshing as I splashed it over my face, scrubbing with sand to clean the stubborn spots on my hands. I freed my hair from its braids and combed it out with my fingers before trapping it once again in a long, single braid. Feeling more presentable, I looked down at my dress, knowing I could do little to help it after sleeping on the ground. Never had I worn the same dress for two days straight.

The men had arrived at this point and were setting up camp, calling it an early night. Other than the setting sun, the only light was a small fire for cooking. The scent of smoke filled the air as one of the men pulled something out of his pack and speared it on a few sticks. The men milled around the small fire, whittling at twigs with their knives or re-bandaging their friends' wounds. Like Ballard said, most of the wounds were minor and non-life-threatening, making me once again feel relieved to see that everyone was all right and still alive.

"*Cass, I am going hunting. I will be back once I have eaten,*" Vasin informed me as he lumbered into the woods.

"*Please be careful,*" I said, reaching out with my thoughts.

"*Everything will be fine. Have no fear, Cass.*"

Feeling calmer about him leaving, I perched on a fallen tree that overlooked the water and watched the fish darting about. I was so engrossed in what I was watching, I nearly fell into the water when someone thrust a meat-covered stick in front of my face.

"You are far too easy to sneak up on." Cole grinned at me as I tried to calm my racing heart.

"Do you take joy in stealing a year off of a person's life with a stunt like that?" I asked, irritated.

"No... just you. Besides, I was being nice by saving you some dinner. If you're going to be nasty about it, I'll just eat it myself." He huffed as he turned away from me and started to walk back to the fire.

"Wait!" I called, hopping off the branch to run after him, snatching the stick out of his hand.

"What is it?" I asked, sniffing the meat, unsure if I really wanted to know the answer.

"It's food," he snapped. "You can eat it or not, but it's all we have for a mouse like you."

Done dealing with me, he made his way back to the fire. Irritated with how he kept treating me, I stuck my tongue out at him but sucked it back in quickly when he looked over his shoulder. He raised an eyebrow at me, letting me know I hadn't been quick enough. This time I just sniffed at him, turning my back and hoping he would trip and fall over something.

I lifted the meat stick to my nose, sniffing it once again, but I couldn't smell anything other than the smoke from the fire. I tore a small piece off and nibbled on it carefully. I was surprised at the flavor and quickly shoved the rest of the chunk in my mouth. It was then that I realized I hadn't eaten since yesterday morning. No wonder Vasin was hungry, and he'd been the one doing all the work. I finished the meat quickly and still felt hungry, so I wandered over to the campfire and sat down with the others. Everyone went silent as I settled myself, watching me with interest. I felt I needed to break the silence but didn't know how.

"Did you get enough to eat, Lady Cassarah?" Richard asked casually.

"Yes, thank you," I lied, since asking for seconds was highly improper. "Could you tell me what that was? It was delicious."

The men all grinned and chuckled a little, looking at each other. I had a feeling I was going to regret asking this question.

"I'm glad that you liked it. Rat is an acquired taste for most," Richard answered.

Instinctively, I covered my mouth to keep from retching up what I just ate. This caused all the men to laugh heartily at my expense. I smiled, knowing I'd reacted just as they expected a noble lady would. It lightened the mood considerably, and the men relaxed and started to tell stories about other strange things they'd eaten.

I laughed as they took delight in telling me all the gruesome details of their experiences. Cole was the only one who sat outside the group and kept silent the entire night, but no one seemed to try and include him, either.

All the men abruptly sprang to their feet, holding knives they'd pulled out of various places. I looked around to see what caught their attention, but I couldn't see anything. Then I heard the strong wing beats of a dragon coming from above.

"*Vasin, is that you?*" I asked silently.

"*YES, I HAVE RETURNED.*"

"It's all right. It's just Vasin coming back from hunting," I shared.

They seemed to relax a little at this news but were still on high alert as he landed on the far edge of the reservoir.

"I don't think I'll ever be used to having a damn dragon around," one of the guys commented.

"I feel blessed. Seeing the black dragon with my own eyes is a rare occurrence. No one alive can say they've seen one," another stated.

"I'm just glad that fucking monster is on our side," I heard someone mutter under their breath.

I whipped around, anger pulsing through my veins as I searched for the man who'd just spoken. Unable to pinpoint who it was, I stood up, getting everyone's attention.

"Listen up, assholes, I will only say this once. That *thing* over there has a name. It's Vasin. I expect you to treat him with the utmost respect. Talking to him is like talking directly to me. I know everything he knows and hear all he hears. Trust me when I say you don't want to be on the receiving end of our wrath."

The shocked men glanced between me and Vasin, who'd silently moved to sit near us, the fire giving his scales an eerie glow. It seemed my words had made their point but killed any chance of returning to the friendly atmosphere. Deciding it was better to leave, I walked over to Vasin and hugged his snout, rubbing my cheek against his scales.

"I think you may have gone a little too far, Cass," Vasin chided as he settled for the night.

"I will never let anyone disrespect you, ever," I grumbled, feeling guilty for lashing out.

Vasin just hummed a little in response. I felt his happiness that I'd stood up for him. Wrapping my arms around his neck, I was yet again surprised by how soft and smooth his scales were.

"They will harden as I age, becoming so strong the sharpest arrow will bounce off. Sadly, that will take years. Right now, I am at my most vulnerable. I can't even breathe fire yet," Vasin shared, picking up on my thoughts.

"Then why is your chest so warm?" I asked, letting go of his snout.

"That is the heat from my embers where the fire comes from. When we are young, the embers are small and not strong enough to ignite the gas we produce. I may look fully grown, but I have much to grow into."

I opened my mouth to ask another question, but Vasin playfully snapped his teeth at me, letting me know he was done talking. He then nudged me with his head toward his raised wing.

"Are you telling me to go to bed?" I laughed.

Another gentle shove and an approving croon told me I was getting the right idea. I noticed he'd already made a pile of leaves for me to sleep on. I smiled at him and scratched under his wing joint he couldn't get to very easily, and he hummed in pleasure. Snuggling into the leaves, I curled against his warm chest and drifted off into a peaceful sleep.

ALMOST HOME

"Lady Cassarah, it is time for us to head out," Ballard called, penetrating my dreamless sleep.

Vasin lifted his protective wing and tucked it back by his side, letting the cool morning air rush in. It reminded me of when Becka used to pull the covers off me when I refused to get out of bed. Slowly, I sat up and glanced around at the camp, only to see that it'd been packed up. Surprised, I blinked a few times and looked up at the sky to see a dim glow from the early morning sunlight. *How early was it?*

"Ballard let you sleep as long as possible, but the rest have been up for some time already," Vasin explained.

Feeling self-conscious, I stood up and shook out my dress, trying to make it look like I hadn't been wearing it for the last three days. Seeing my efforts were useless, I gave up and walked to the reservoir to wash my face. I might be living in the forest, but I didn't need to look like a wild beast. I gasped when I saw my blurred reflection on the water's surface. It seemed all the leaves that I'd been sleeping on ended up knotted in my hair.

I quickly unbraided my hair and shook out as many leaves as possible. What I wouldn't give for a hot bath at this moment. I was trying to make the best of this but was sick and tired of living in these conditions. I was a proper lady and their queen, or so they claimed. How could I meet the clan members looking like this? Who would want some wild wretch to be their queen? Hurriedly, I combed my fingers through my hair, attempting to tame the wild curls that had come to life with a mind all their own.

"Here, before you scare the horses," Cole said as he thrust a simple wooden comb in my face.

I frowned as I took it. "Is this the only kind of brush you have?"

"If you don't want to use it, fine. Hand it over and look like the mouse you act like," Cole growled out, trying to grab the comb out of my hand.

I slapped his hand away, pulling the comb close so he couldn't grab it. "It was a simple question, no need to get so upset."

"Women," Cole grumbled, marching away from me, tossing up his hands.

Raking the comb through my hair, I tamed it into a single braid and wrapped it into a bun, pinning it in place with a sturdy twig. Finally ready, I walked back to the smothered campfire where everyone else was waiting. The men watched me cautiously as if they were still deciding what to make of me after my outburst.

"Today, you're going to ride with me," Ballard informed me, breaking the silence my arrival had caused.

"We will make it there by night?" I asked, excited that this part of the journey was ending so soon.

"Yes, if the weather holds out, we should get there before nightfall, and you'll have a proper bed to sleep in tonight."

"Are you sure I can't just fly? Vasin holds the memories of all the past dragons, so I'm sure he knows the location already," I said, not loving the idea of riding double all day.

"We've moved locations many times since a dragon last graced our clan. Where his memories would take him is no longer accurate," Ballard explained. "Once we get to our current location, you will be able to share that information with him."

I looked over at Vasin. *"Is he right? Can you find us once I'm there?"*

"Yes, now that we have harmonized, I will always be able to find you."

"Very well." I sighed, knowing it would be a long day. "I'm ready when you are."

"Don't sound so glum. Tonight you will be sleeping in your new home and even be able to take a bath," Ballard said, giving me a warm smile.

My heart sank a little as he mentioned the word 'home.' I hadn't had much time to think about the fact that other than these strangers, I didn't have a home to go back to. My parents had been okay with letting my dragon die to save their reputation. I'd always assumed my father would be on my side when Mother crossed the line, but sadly, the honest truth was shown to me that night in the library. My father made his priorities known, and I was not one of them. Sobered with this truth, I took Ballard's outstretched hand and was pulled up behind him on his horse.

We silently journeyed through the mountains, and I was amazed at its strange beauty. It was like nothing I'd ever seen before in my sheltered life. Every living thing fought for its place here—nothing was given freely. I could see why the mercenaries chose to make their home here—few could withstand the tests that it doled out, keeping them safe.

A harsh wind twined its way through sparse, stunted trees and all that grew on this part of the mountain's peak. I buried my face into Ballard's warm, wool-cloaked back, trying to use him as a shield to block the wind. No matter what I did, though, the wind always seemed to find me, chilling me to the core. Somehow, it felt like the wind was alive and testing to see if I was strong enough to survive on its mountain, worthy of its protection.

Finally, we descended deeper into the lower regions of the mountain, the wind losing its biting power amidst the thick pine trees.

Ballard led us confidently down paths an untrained eye would never see. I was glad they hadn't made me find this place on my own, or I would've been lost forever in the woods. We briefly stopped for a simple meal of dried meat and thick flatbread, and strangely, no one seemed willing to speak, even now as we rested. Was there some danger I didn't know about? No, Vasin would have told me if he saw anything following us.

"Saddle up. We have the final stretch ahead of us, then we're home, boys," Ballard said with a grin.

The men laughed quietly and elbowed each other, showing the first signs of the men they'd been last night. Yet as soon as they were mounted, not another word or sound was uttered. My attention was pulled away from my musings when we exited the thick forest and abruptly found ourselves on the edge of a cliff. I thought we'd taken a wrong turn somewhere and were now lost because there was nowhere to go but back the way we came.

I should've known not to doubt Ballard, but you had to wonder when your fearless leader sent you off a cliff.

"Ballard, are you trying to kill us?" I whispered harshly as I fisted the back of his cloak. Ignoring me, he kept his horse moving and stepped off the cliff to our death—or so I thought.

Large steps had been cut into the side of the mountain, hidden from view unless you knew they were there. Even though I *knew* the steps were there, I couldn't keep my eyes open for fear I might scream at the sheer plummet of death on my right side.

"We've safely made it across. You can relax now," Ballard murmured, followed by a chuckle.

I opened my eyes to see we had indeed crossed to the other side of the huge ravine that would have normally taken two or three days to cross. I looked back, and even aware there were indeed steps, they were impossible to see from this angle. How in the world had they managed to carve those? These mercenaries gained more and more respect in my eyes. I never imagined there could be such skilled people in the world.

True to his word, the worst was over. We traveled swiftly down smooth, packed trails that looked well-used. I also noticed that the men started to speak to one another in soft-spoken conversations, but there was a more relaxed feel to our surroundings than before.

"How much farther is it?" I asked.

"We should be home very shortly. We made good time since the weather was clear."

I pictured making the journey in the rain or snow and shivered. I'd never have been able to survive without them in those conditions. It just reminded me once again how much I needed to learn to be of any help to these people.

The ground was softer than before, covered in grass instead of the harsh shrubs of the higher mountain region. The trees overhead grew thick and close together, creating a ceiling of leaves. Suddenly, Ballard brought his horse to an abrupt stop, and unprepared for it, I crashed into his back, almost unseating myself.

I peered around Ballard's body to see a man standing in the middle of the forest holding a bow at the ready. "If you're looking to pass, you have to pay the price."

"Credit is better than money, my friend," Ballard called as he tossed back the hood of his cloak.

The man laughed and lowered his bow. "Truer words were never spoken, ye old goat. Glad to see you and the boys made it back safe. Did you succeed in your plans?"

"She's riding behind me. I'll introduce her to you all later. It's been a long trip back."

"Of course." With that, the man let out a shrill whistle, and a moment later, a hidden gate that blended into the forest was opened. "Welcome home, boys."

I watched in awe at the transformation once we passed through the gate. The woods seem to fall away into a huge open meadow with sheep and goats grazing in large pens. Simple wooden houses arranged in a large circle had smoke drifting out of chimneys, sending pungent smells of the dinners they cooked through the air. In the middle of the circle of houses was a large building two stories high, equaling three of the other homes. This was the building we all stopped in front of. Ballard helped me to dismount first, then he swung down.

The men who opened the gate must have sent word ahead because all the families were soon pouring out of the houses and racing over to us. Some of the men I traveled with raced to catch small children in their arms. Others just led the horses behind the large building, presumably in the direction of the stables. A slender older woman with silver hair tied loosely back from her face walked up to Ballard and hugged him fiercely. I never thought about the fact that Ballard might have a wife. It wasn't long before I was the one clasped in a tight hug by the same woman, trying not to flinch under the unfamiliar contact.

"Welcome to our clan and your new home! I can only imagine what you've gone through to get here, and I'm very thankful you did it. Come, you must be hungry and tired. You also look in want of a proper bath." Without even giving her name, she whisked me away from the crowd and into the large building.

The first level of the building looked like a large meeting room that could hold everyone in the clan, a large wooden chair carved with intricate designs at the front. Ballard's wife led me through the room and into the large kitchen, which featured a huge hearth with room for three large cooking pots to be used all at once. A smaller pot was hung over the fire, filling the room with its savory aroma. I was placed at a long wooden table with benches on either side and promptly served with a bowl of stew and soft, flaky bread.

"Now that's better. Eat your fill while we heat the water for your bath," she said, smiling warmly at me.

I nodded, thrown off by the kindness she was giving me. I was more accustomed to the disdain the other Norden nobles tended to throw our way.

I tentatively scooped some of the stew, unsure of what could be in it, and sniffed. I wanted to ask, but I held my tongue as my mouth began to water uncontrollably. I sipped from the spoon, and that was all I needed to know before quickly finishing the bowl. Ballard's wife and one other woman came back into the kitchen carrying a large cast iron pot filled to the brim with water. I was amazed at how effortlessly they carried such a heavy pot and hooked it over the fire to heat.

"I'm glad to see you like the stew. Would you like another bowl?" Ballard's wife asked.

My cheeks heated with embarrassment because I so badly wanted to be gluttonous and say yes. Thankfully, my stomach growled and gave me away, and without me having to say a word, my bowl was filled once again. This time she sat down across from me and smiled, her soft brown eyes showing it was genuine. I instantly felt safe with this woman, who seemed to give off comfort and love in everything she did.

"I'm so glad you decided to come here to live with us. I feel as though a huge weight has been lifted from our shoulders."

I choked on the food I was swallowing, surprised by this woman's candor and directness. We hadn't even exchanged names yet, and she was already talking to me like family. She quickly stood up and thwacked me on the back, helping me catch my breath, which sent me into another fit at the shock of being hit by a stranger like it was totally normal.

"Now, now, no need to get all excited," she cooed. Once I was all right, she sat back down.

"Thank you..." I said, hoping this would trigger her to tell me her name.

"Goodness, it seems I've completely lost my manners. We don't have guests in these parts of the mountain very often. My name is Helena, and as you have already guessed, I'm Ballard's wife."

"I'm Cassarah, daughter of Baron Charles and Baroness Adeline of Norden. It's a pleasure to meet you," I parroted perfectly, just as I was taught.

"My, my, what the proper lady you are. Goodness, people are going to have to get used to that, I'm afraid." Helena giggled.

"Please don't," I said, automatically reaching out to grasp her arm. "I want to learn to be more like everyone else. They need me to adjust to and understand them, not the other way around."

"Well, aren't you full of surprises," Helena said, patting my hand. "Let's leave that talk for tomorrow. For now, let's get you washed up and into a proper bed."

It was at that moment it struck me I hadn't called for Vasin yet. He was waiting alone in the mountains for me to reach out to him.

"I have to find Ballard first. Vasin's alone and waiting for me. He's vulnerable right now and can't be left defenseless in the mountains," I cried out, beginning to panic. How could I have forgotten him so easily?

"Calm down, child. I'm sure he's fine. I'll send for Ballard, and he'll help you figure all this out," Helena said, grabbing my hand and giving it a reassuring squeeze.

I began to panic, unsure if I could reach him from here. We'd traveled so far from where we'd left him to wait. Previously, I couldn't even reach him from my home to the castle, and this was easily three times that distance. I closed my eyes, reaching deep to find that thread of connection Vasin and I shared. Panicking, I grasped that stronger connection rather than relying on our mental link. Upon harmonizing, I was immediately swallowed by that strange, warm sensation that let me leave my body and join with Vasin's.

"*CASS, WHY ARE YOU HERE LIKE THIS? YOU SHOULDN'T USE THIS POWER UNLESS I AM CLOSE BY TO PROTECT YOU,*" Vasin scolded.

"*I didn't know if I could reach you by calling. I was worried I wouldn't be able to find you.*"

"*I SENSE YOUR WORRY, BUT YOU MUST UNDERSTAND THAT USING THIS POWER LEAVES YOUR BODY LIKE AN EMPTY SHELL, VULNERABLE TO ANYTHING. SINCE YOU ARE ALREADY HERE, I WILL GO AHEAD AND TAKE THE LOCATION FROM YOUR MEMORIES. WHILE I DO THIS, YOU MUSTN'T LOOK DEEPER INTO MY MIND. THE INFORMATION CONTAINED HERE IS MORE THAN ANY HUMAN CAN COMPREHEND.*"

"*I understand.*"

The sensation of Vasin looking into my memories was a strange feeling but not altogether unpleasant. It felt as if a soft wind was blowing over me, combined with a nagging feeling that someone was watching me from some unseen place.

As he sought the information he needed, I caught sight of something from the corner of my eye that looked vaguely familiar. I couldn't place why it was familiar or even tell you what it was. All I knew was I had to find out why it was here.

I could feel myself being drawn deeper, all the while something in the back of my mind cautioning me that this was a bad idea. Yet the urge to know was greater than any fear or warning. Just as I was within reach of it, everything changed. A torrent of flashing colors came first, followed by being bombarded with memories, emotions, and sounds I'd never experienced before. I could feel my brain trying to figure everything out and failing to understand. I felt as if I would explode from all the stimulants, but I didn't know how to escape it.

"CASSARAH, WHAT HAVE YOU DONE? I TOLD YOU NOT TO ENTER DEEPER INTO MY MEMORIES. QUICK, TRY AND CLOSE YOUR MIND BEFORE IT'S TOO LATE. THINK OF YOUR BODY, WHERE YOU WERE LAST, WHAT YOU WERE LAST DOING. QUICKLY NOW, OR YOU'LL BE LOST HERE FOREVER!"

I tried to do as he said, thinking of the large kitchen I'd just been sitting in with Helena. I tried to remember what it felt like to have my hands resting on the well-worn wood, the smell of the stew, the taste of it. No matter what I thought about, I couldn't seem to get a grasp on my real body. It felt like I was being torn in all directions. Just when I thought I was done for, I heard someone calling my name.

"Cassarah, wake up!" Cole's voice pierced through the chaos, giving me something to latch onto. "I did not traipse all over God's green earth to find you just to have you die without doing anything helpful. Dammit, woman, wake the hell up."

I felt something connect to my face, the sting of what could only be a slap. Anger rose inside me in response. I could feel the power of my Birthright pulling me back into my body, ready for a fight. I opened my eyes to find that the room was flooded with a pale blue light that seemed to dissipate as my eyes cleared. Cole looked down at me with an irritated frown while Helena was wiping tears from her face.

"If I'd known you were going to be this much work, I would've left your ass in Norden," Cole said before he stood up and left the room.

"Vasin is on his way," I croaked out before he disappeared through the doorway.

TEN

MEET THE CLAN

"*Miranda, come down out of that tree! The clan emissaries are here," my mother called from below.*

"I'm not coming down. You can't make me."

"Young lady, if you think I can't knock you out of that tree, you are more foolish than I thought."

I glanced down to see my mother aiming her slingshot, making her threat known. I could come down on my own or become target practice. Huffing, I clambered down the tree and landed at my mother's side.

"Look at you... you're filthy. What will your guards and possible consorts think of the wild creature they are to one day marry?"

"I'm not getting married, Mother. I'm going to be a great warrior queen and rule over our people with Cheery by my side. I don't need anyone but her."

My mother rolled her eyes at me, having fought this battle many times before. "Miranda, the connection between you and your dragon is important, but the bond between a woman and the man or men she loves is something just as magical."

"What if I don't like any of them? You keep telling me I'm free to choose who I want. What if I only like three out of the five of them?"

"We will cross that bridge when we get there. Eventually, you will find someone you can't live without, even if it's not these five particular boys. That is why you will all train together so you can get to know each of them. You can't marry until you're eighteen, so we have a few years left before it's time to decide."

"They won't want to marry me if I beat their asses in training."

"I don't know... your father found that very endearing about me."

"Ew, Mother, I don't want to hear about that."

My mother laughed as we headed off to meet the leaders from the other clans.

As the dream ended and my body woke, it ached from head to toe. Opening my eyes, I found myself in a large bed in a neatly furnished room. A cheerful fire blazed in a large fireplace, heating the space and giving off a soft glow. Looking out one of the few windows, I saw it was still night out. Had I only been asleep for a short while? For some reason, it felt like it'd been much longer. A soft knock sounded on the door before it was slowly opened, and Helena walked in, holding a tray.

Helena sighed with relief when she saw me. "Oh, thank the heavens you're finally awake."

"How long have I been asleep?" I rasped, my throat dry.

"You've been asleep almost two days with barely a stir. We had the doctor check on you, and he kept telling us there was nothing wrong, that you just needed time. I guess that old coot was right for once," Helena said as she took the cover off a bowl of soup and a large piece of bread.

Upon seeing the food, my stomach growled loudly, causing me to blush. It's not like I hadn't gone two days without food before. I heaved myself up to lean against the wooden headboard as Helena gently placed the tray of food on my lap. The soup was piping hot and exactly what I needed to feel like myself again. The warmth soothed my tight muscles, and I let out a sigh of contentment.

"That's better," Helena said as she sat on the edge of my bed. "What on earth happened to you, child?"

"I went far too deep into Vasin's memories when we harmonized. Then I couldn't pull myself out of them," I explained, but when I saw the question on her face, I tried to describe it better. "Each dragon can access all the memories of their ancestors. The knowledge they possess is overwhelming for any human to withstand. Unfortunately, I touched what I shouldn't have."

"Ah." Helena nodded. "Well, it looks like we're going to need to start your education as soon as possible. Our ancestors who were chosen by the black dragon wrote down all the information they learned to share with those to come. Much like dragons do for each other, only less dangerous."

"Wait, so others have been able to talk to their dragon? I'm not the only one?"

"Oh, heavens no, child. All our kings and queens have been able to do that. It's what makes them such wonderful leaders. They have all that vast knowledge of their dragon at their fingertips to help advise them."

My mouth gaped open. Not only was I going to have access to knowledge that would help me figure all this out, but I wasn't crazy for talking to my dragon!

My reaction must have been a sight, for it sent Helena into a laughing fit. "Child, you look like I just handed you a new silk dress! Trust me, when you start your royal training, you won't be so happy about it."

After she calmed herself from her laughter, she stood up and gestured over to a trunk in the corner. "That's filled with all the things you'll need starting tomorrow. Everyone in the clans is given the exact same items when they start training because no one here is more important than another when on a job."

I nodded as a wave of tiredness washed over me. "I guess I should take advantage of my last time to sleep as much as I want," I said wistfully to myself as Helena shut the door quietly behind her.

"*Vasin, are you there?*" I asked, wondering if he was mad at me.

"*Yes, Cass, I am here. Are you feeling all right?*"

"*I think so. I had the craziest dream, though. It was like I was watching a memory of something in the past. Could some of the memories I tapped into still be rolling around in my head?*"

"*It could be. No one has survived that much knowledge at once before. I thought I was going to lose you.*" I could feel his worry through our bond.

"*I won't be doing that again any time soon, promise. And I'm sorry I didn't listen,*" I apologized, trying to reassure him as I drifted off into a dreamless sleep.

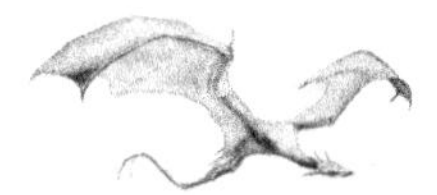

"M'lady, it's time for you to get up," a strange woman said. "Ballard is going to introduce you to the clan this morning."

I moved slowly as two other women brought in a tub and began filling it with large steaming buckets of water. Again, I was amazed at the strength these women had to easily lift each bucket like it was filled with feathers. I had a distinct feeling that everyone pulled their weight around here, and I too would be just as strong.

Gingerly, I slipped into the water and hummed as my body relaxed and muscles loosened.

"Would you like us to wash you up? They are expecting you rather quick-like," one of the ladies asked, rolling up her sleeves.

The thought of having a stranger washing me sent shivers down my spine. Becka had been the only one I'd allowed to do that for me. After all of the beatings, I didn't feel comfortable with being that vulnerable if I could help it.

"Thank you, but I'll be faster doing it myself." Then I swiftly washed my hair, rinsing it with the pitcher of water they'd left for me. Once clean, I hopped out and dried myself off, my skin reacting to the chill in the fall air.

Opening the chest, I found an assortment of clothing and basic supplies, including a wooden comb. Raking it through my damp hair, I braided it tightly to my head, letting the tail fall down my back. As I rifled through the chest again, trying to decide what to wear, I noticed something strange. There were no skirts, only soft leather pants in different shades of brown and black. I pulled out a pair and looked at them, intrigued. Was I allowed to wear these? Helena had said everything I needed would be in here, so I guessed I'd give it a try.

After dressing, I looked at myself in the mirror hanging on the wall by the wash bowl. The leather pants were soft and more comfortable than I thought possible, and the simple white tunic was covered by a fitted leather top that tightened on the sides. Knowing I didn't have to wear a corset anymore was so freeing.

"M'lady, are you ready?" Ballard called from outside the door.

In answer, I opened the door and smiled at him. He took a moment to look me over, a little surprised at my new attire.

"How do I look?" I asked, feeling unsure.

"You look like you were born to be one of us, m'lady." Ballard smiled as he dipped his head in a small bow.

"Please, don't call me that," I pleaded. "I'm no longer a noble lady of the court."

"Very well, Cassarah, but once you officially take over ruling the clans, no one will be this informal," Ballard warned.

Silently, we walked down the stairs and along a short hallway with one door at the end. It opened into the kitchen, which surprised me because I didn't remember a door there before. Sure enough, now that I was looking for it, the door was hidden in the wood paneling.

"That doorway is the only one that leads to your bedroom. There is another staircase off the meeting room that leads to the rest of the rooms where my family lives, but yours is in a different section. If we ever got attacked, they would never be able to find it," Ballard explained.

These mercenaries really loved hiding things in plain sight and were good at it.

Ballard started walking to the meeting hall and stopped before the door. "I'll walk up with you to the front and introduce you to the people. They will have many questions, but please let me answer them. I just need you to be strong and stand fearlessly by my side. It's been a long time since our people have had a king or queen, and some are not taking to it well."

I blinked at him, surprised by this information, but I stood up a little straighter and stuck my chin out like my mother taught me. "I can do that."

Ballard squeezed my shoulder reassuringly before he opened the door and walked through it with me close behind. The murmuring hum of conversation stopped when they saw us. Some smiled and waved at me, while others sat there blank-faced and stony-eyed. When we got to the front of the hall, we stood side by side in front of the ornate wooden chair I assumed was the throne.

"Thank you all for coming this morning. I know the meeting was called on short notice. As many of you know, the black dragon has chosen a new leader. What you don't know is that Lady Cassarah is born of this clan, though she has no knowledge of us. Many of you remember the tale of betrayal we suffered when Alister traded us for a title and land. Well, this is his great-great-granddaughter, Cassarah, who is pair-bonded to the black dragon, Vasin."

The room burst into chaos upon hearing this. Some were shouting their disapproval while others sat stunned. I was in the latter group. I'd never heard much about my family's past, and the story Ballard told hadn't been what I expected. Father had said something about the clan disowning the family, but I'd assumed that was because one of my grandfathers had simply left and chosen Norden and the title over the mercenaries—not that he'd actively betrayed them.

"How can we have a traitor's offspring be our queen?" one woman shouted.

"We need a leader we can trust! Our people are being picked off by the King's Guard. Hardly any of us are left at this point. We need someone who will save us, not someone we have to worry about running away," another man called out.

"I know you're all unsure of this. I was myself, as well, until I met her and spent some time with her. Cassarah has decided to go through training just like all of you and your children have done for generations."

This seemed to get people's attention.

Wait!? When had we decided I was going to mercenary school? The only thing Helena had mentioned was 'royal' training. Now I felt like I was being played.

"Cassarah will be trained in all our ways on top of her learning the queen's duties. If she hasn't shown herself a worthy asset in one year, then she will not become our queen. Instead, she will remain here with us under our watchful eye with her dragon keeping us safe," Ballard explained.

This silenced everyone immediately, and they all looked at me for the first time. *What the hell! Did he mean I would be an outcast if I couldn't do this? Why wouldn't they just let me be free to live my life?*

I gulped, trying not to show my fear and anger at the trap I'd walked into. How was I going to pull this off? Could I really learn to be one of them in a year, learning to do all the things they'd been training for since they were children?

"Does anyone object to this proposal?" Ballard asked calmly.

No one responded, signaling their agreement with silence.

"Very well, then. You may all go about your day unless you have other matters to discuss with the clan."

Slowly, everyone filed out of the room until it was just Ballard and me.

"What the hell did you just promise them?" I demanded, turning on Ballard. I was shaking with anger, fists clenched, trying to keep from punching him in the face. I felt betrayed and used. He was no different than my mother at this point.

"It's the only way to get them to respect you, Cassarah," Ballard said, turning to me.

"You have no right to do this to me!" I snarled. "You lied to me! You let me believe that I was wanted, even needed! Your people don't even want a queen, do they? They want a general who will lead them into war, and that's not me. Oh, and what's this crap about that if I can't do this, I'll be a pariah in your world? Who are you to barter with my life or my dragon's?"

Ballard looked down at me, his eyes gentle but firm. "I'm the regent of this clan, and I *will* do what is best for my people. You are one of them now, Cassarah, whether you see it or not."

"How can I be one of your people if you're willing to set me up for failure?"

"Are you so ready to believe you'll fail before you even try?"

I didn't answer right away, still replaying his betrayal. The stubborn part of me didn't want to back down from the challenge, but the part that had been beaten for standing up for myself shrank at the idea.

"I guess I don't have a choice now, do I?"

"You always have a choice, but I wish you'd try. This is going to be a long, hard road, but worth it in the end, I promise you."

"No one should promise things they can't guarantee, Ballard," I said, walking out of the meeting room to stand on the porch. Maybe the sunlight would chase away my fears.

ELEVEN

EMOTIONAL OVERLOAD

"Let's start today by showing you around our village," Ballard said. "I'll also need to introduce you to our recordkeeper, Sal. He never leaves his home, so he's never at the meetings."

The cabins in the clearing were just a small part of the Raven Rose clan that was tucked into the surrounding woods. The records hall was a cozy two-story wooden building stuffed with all sorts of papers, scrolls, and books. The roof had four hatches propped open, letting the afternoon light fill the place. An old man sat at a desk strewn with papers, intently reading and jotting down notes. He didn't even notice us until Ballard cleared his throat loudly, breaking the silence.

"Oh, Ballard! What can I help you with today?" the older man said as he stood up and walked over to us.

"Sal, I would like to introduce you to Lady Cassarah, pair-bond to the black dragon, Vasin," Ballard said formally.

Sal peered at me, squinting his eyes. "I see, so this is the new queen. I assume you brought her here to start her training. Is she literate?" he asked, turning to Ballard. Then he seemed to reconsider. "I apologize.

She was raised as a noble lady. I should've asked can she read and write more than her name?"

There were many things I had learned to take in silence, but I couldn't keep quiet when it came to my intelligence. I was proud of the knowledge I'd earned and wouldn't let anyone look down at me.

"As a matter of fact, *she* can read and write her name in three different languages, thank you very much," I snapped.

Sal turned back to me, his face unreadable. "Just your name? That is a pretty trick but not all that useful."

I bristled at his words. The fact I knew three languages was unheard of for a woman. "I'm fluent in all three."

Sal simply nodded, clasped his hands behind his back, and walked over to a bookcase, ignoring me. I looked at Ballard, but he watched silently as the older man pulled books off the shelf. Sal then walked back to me, thrusting three books and two scrolls into my hands.

"Read these, then come back to me in two days. We will see how much you actually understand," Sal said before walking back to his desk, sitting down, and ignoring us.

Ballard grabbed my arm to lead me out, and I flinched at his touch. He let go of me instantly and motioned for me to follow him.

"What's up with that old man?" I asked, exasperated, after we'd walked a little ways from his house.

"Sal's memorized everything in that library. He's the one we go to when we need advice. He will be an invaluable asset to you when you take the throne. I would learn all you can from him while he is still with us. He's training an apprentice to take over for him, but she is young and doesn't have his wisdom."

"I get that, but why must he be so rude? I didn't do anything to deserve that kind of treatment."

"You're an outsider, and that's all it takes for some. Sal, especially, because he never sets foot outside that building and doesn't know much about the real world," Ballard explained, stopping to look at me. "You're going to meet many people, and some may warm up to you, but most will assume the worst. Are you prepared to handle that?"

"Once again, I'm left with no choice in the matter. If I ever want to be treated like I belong, I have to find a way to deal with the cold shoulder," I answered honestly.

"True enough. Come on, let's go meet your horse."

I smiled at that. "Now that is something I already know how to do."

"Can you ride astride or just sidesaddle?"

"Sidesaddle."

Ballard nodded and kept walking, not needing to say what I already knew. Sidesaddle would do me no good here.

We approached a long, low building full of stalls, but only a few had horses standing in them. Ballard walked over to a stall with a regal-looking black mare observing us as we walked up.

"This is Inali. She will be yours once you've been fully trained to ride. She is specifically trained as a mercenary horse and knows all the trick riding you'll ever need," Ballard said, then walked to the next stall where a sweet chestnut mare thrust her head into his chest. "This is Grace, and she will be who you'll learn from. Once you've mastered the basics, you'll be taught everything else with Inali."

"Trick riding?" I questioned.

"I'll let you find out about that when the time comes... no sense in overwhelming you with too much information. Come on... this is the arena where you'll learn your combat skills."

"Combat?" I blurted. Proper ladies never learned how to fight.

"We're not like the nobility who seem to think the fairer sex is stupid and unable to learn. Some of our best members have been women. They have skills that men could never achieve."

"What kind of combat am I going to learn?" Hopefully, it would just be something basic.

"We'll begin with archery, swordsmanship, knife fighting, and hand-to-hand. Once you have learned those, we'll move onto the specialized skills."

My mouth fell open in shock at how calmly Ballard explained this to me. Who could learn all of this in one year?

"Who is going to be teaching me all this?"

"You'll have a few different teachers, but Cole will teach you archery, knife fighting, and other basic skills. Abbott will teach you swordsmanship, hand-to-hand combat, and overall body conditioning. Your horsemanship teacher isn't back yet but should be along shortly. Once they feel you're ready, your final test will be the same as the other trainees. You will be sent on a job and evaluated on how well you do."

"You must be joking. You can't really think I'll be able to do all this in a year and survive on a real job! I might as well give up now. I'm not cut out for this kind of thing," I declared, panicking at the overwhelming task.

All I could hear was my mother telling me I would never be good enough. How many beatings and lessons did it take to figure out where my proper place was in life? This was a dream, and there was no way I could manage to accomplish this all in a year. I hadn't been able to become a perfect, proper lady, and I'd had twenty-one years of training for that.

"Is that really how you view yourself? Worthless of even trying?" Ballard asked, sadness showing in his eyes.

"What makes you so sure that I'd be any good as a queen for your people? Why do you keep pushing this on me?"

Not waiting for his answer, I tossed the books and scrolls at Ballard's feet and ran out the door and into the woods. I ran as fast as I could, tears blurring my vision. I knew I was taking the coward's way out, but I couldn't handle being a failure again. It was too much for me to bear. I wasn't just failing my mother this time, I would be failing a whole group of people.

Finally, I stopped and collapsed on the soft, leaf-covered ground, gasping for breath. I didn't know how far I'd run, but my burning lungs told me it was quite a ways.

"Cass."

I looked up and found Vasin standing in a small clearing of trees right in front of me. I stood, rushing at him, then threw my arms around his neck.

"Cass, tell me what's the matter? Your pain is overwhelming our connection. Are you hurt? I came to you as soon as I could."

When I didn't answer, Vasin curled his wings around us to create our private hideaway. He cradled me between his front legs, the warmth from his chest comforting me as I sobbed.

For years, I'd never let myself cry, having wasted so many tears pleading with my stone-faced mother. Now they refused to be held back. I cried for all those times Mother told them to whip me, bridled me for days on end, beat Becka, and made me feel utterly worthless. I was free from her clutches, but her words still haunted me, even so many miles away.

"I can't do this. I'm not fit to be anyone's queen. I'm not strong enough to do this. I'm worthless, a total disappointment. Everything

I do is wrong, and nothing good ever happens to me. I'm always being used, even if it hurts me."

"Does that include me?"

"Of course not," I said, horrified at the thought.

"Are you willing to trust me? Even with your life?"

I looked up at him, gazing into his bright, intelligent eyes, and nodded. "I trust you completely."

"Then trust in the fact I chose you. I know you will be the best queen these people will ever have. I've seen their past, and you are exactly what they need right now. You were always meant to lead these people to prosperity and freedom. I need you to believe that too, or all will be lost." Vasin pulled back his wings and nudged me with his nose. *"Now dry your tears, and I will take you back to the village."*

"I don't think I can go back there. You should've seen the look on Ballard's face. He might be second-guessing his choice for the queen."

"I doubt that. He has led these people all by himself for many years. I am sure he understands the challenges you're facing. Now climb on my back. You have run a fair distance from the clan's village."

Moments later, Vasin dropped me off near the edge of the clearing, trying not to draw too much attention to our arrival.

"Thank you, Vasin. I feel much better now. I'm still not sure how this will go, but I trust you." I smiled and scratched him just above the eyelid. He hummed his pleasure and nuzzled me before walking back into the forest.

Taking a deep breath, I made an about-face and readied myself for the conversation Ballard and I were going to have. The front door was left open, so my entry was quiet as I walked into the now-deserted meeting room. I peered around, trying to see if he was here when I heard voices from the kitchen.

"Darling, you have to give her time. Her world just turned upside down. Of course she's scared. I would be too if you asked me to learn a whole new way of life in such a short time," Helena chided.

"I'm trying the best I can, but that family of hers has convinced her she is incapable of doing anything. I know she has it in her. I can see it," Ballard said, the strength of his conviction clear in his voice. "She just needs to believe in her inner strength that I can plainly see."

I felt tears welling up in my eyes. In no way had someone ever believed me capable of achieving anything for myself. Hearing someone put so much faith in me was overwhelming. Vasin, of course, had been right. I wasn't a lost cause to Ballard—he did believe I had it in me to be successful.

"Hey, you just going to stand there all awkward, or are you going into the kitchen any time soon?" Cole's haughty voice snapped me out of my thoughts.

I whirled around, coming face-to-face with him, not realizing how close he'd been standing behind me. I instinctively stepped back, not comfortable with him being in my space. His green eyes watched me with a bored expression, and then he slowly circled me as if sizing me up. I fought the urge to flee from his scrutiny, feeling exposed under his gaze.

"I hear I'm going to teach you some combat skills," he said, facing me again. "I think it's a waste, to be honest. There's no way you'll ever be able to pull this off in a year and survive a job. That being said, if you really want to learn, I will teach you. But if you don't give it your all, I won't be to blame for your failure or death."

I flinched at his words as they cut through me like a knife. They were too close to the words that had filled my head all day. I agreed—I didn't know if I could survive out there on a job.

Then the words Ballard and Vasin said reminded me I had people who thought I could prevail. Anger at Cole's words bloomed in my chest. I'd had it with this boy and his insults about my intelligence, strength, and capabilities. If I were willing to do anything, it would be to show him how wrong he was. I would learn everything I needed in a year, and I would be better than him by the time I'm done.

Cole's haughty look faltered as I came to this decision, and his eyes narrowed as if he could see the change in attitude come over me.

"I would watch how you address me, Cole," I said, looking deep into his eyes so I knew I had his attention. "I will be your queen in a year's time, and I won't forget those who have wronged me along the way. Then who will be the little mouse?"

"This is what I've been saying all along... under that ladylike exterior is steel," Ballard said, grinning in the kitchen doorway. "I would be careful from now on, Cole. I get the feeling she'll be a force to be reckoned with when pissed off."

"Enough of that kind of talk," Helena said, waving us all into the kitchen, a soft smile on her face. "Come sit down, the lot of you, and let's have lunch together. Abbott's still on a job, so we won't see him until tomorrow morning for your first day of training."

"Who is Abbott?" I asked, remembering Ballard saying his name before.

We sat at the large wooden table as Helena set down plates and bowls filled with wonderful-smelling food.

"He was born in one of the other clans, but his parents died. The clan didn't have enough to go around to take care of a newborn, so we took him in," Ballard shared. "He lives in his own cabin but still comes and has his meals with us."

Surreptitiously, I watched what the others did since there weren't any servants to dish out the food. Cole grabbed bread from the basket while Ballard scooped potatoes into his bowl without hesitation. I gingerly plucked a slice of bread out of the basket, trying to make it look like this wasn't my first time.

"Hand me your plate, dear," Helena said, coming to my rescue and filling my plate with the sides.

"Thank you," I said. "It all smells amazing."

"Helena is the best cook in the clan. No one can come close to the food she makes," Cole boasted between mouthfuls. "Wait till you try some of her pies. They are like tasting heaven."

"Don't think I don't know what you're up to with all that flattery, Cole," Helena said, waving a finger at him before she turned back to me. "I am glad you like the food, dear. I wasn't sure if it would measure up to what you are used to eating."

"This food is way better than what our cook back home could make. Although, I think when you're not allowed to eat all the time, you find you're not very picky," I said as I swallowed another spoonful.

They all stopped eating and looked at me with expressions ranging from horror to shock. I hadn't meant to let that slip out, but I was so caught up in the friendly conversation I'd said it without thinking. It made me wonder if this is what a real family meal was supposed to be like. It was vastly different from our stiff and formal meals, where the only sound came from our silverware. I could get used to being surrounded by the gentle flow of conversation and laughter.

"Cassarah, are you all right, dear?" Helena asked, pulling me out of my thoughts.

"I'm fine. The past few days have been a little overwhelming, is all."

"I would think so. Why don't you go up to your room and rest for a while once you're finished eating? Training isn't until tomorrow, so why not take the afternoon to settle in," Helena suggested as she turned to Ballard. "That would be fine, wouldn't it, love?"

Even though she asked the question, I already knew she was telling more than asking.

"I think that's a great idea. I brought the books that Sal gave you and put them in your room if you feel like reading," Ballard commented.

"Thank you for lunch... it was delicious. I think I'm going to take your advice and head up." I stacked my dishes and picked them up but then stopped, a little lost as to what to do with them next.

"Just set them in the wash basin, child. I'll take care of them." She pointed to a large metal basin with a water pump next to it. I bowed my head in thanks and did as she asked, then slid open the secret door to my room.

TWELVE

OBSTACLE COURSE

S itting on the bed, I looked out the window at the bright blue sky and the turning leaves fluttering in the light breeze. My window was open, letting the wind brush across my face, carrying with it the rich scent of the forest.

I closed my eyes and took in the peaceful moment, letting all the day's worries drift away. My mind began to wander, and small flashes of strange memories flitted before my mind's eye. I felt as though I shouldn't be remembering these things like they weren't mine to know. Then the same distant figure appeared in the corner of my eye. Why was it that I kept seeing this apparition in my thoughts? Just when I tried to focus on the image, it blurred out of sight.

I opened my eyes and sighed, frustrated, feeling like I was being teased. Every time I got closer to seeing clearly, it vanished like a ghost.

Catching sight of the books and scrolls on the small table near the window, I pushed myself off the bed and walked over to them, randomly picking up one. The book was a record of the clan's finances for the past several years. It was a very detailed listing of the jobs that had been taken, how many men were required for each, the food and supplies needed, and how much it cost overall. From what I could tell, the clan took half the payment up front, which always covered the cost of food and supplies. Then, when the job was finished, the rest was collected, and the men were paid their share after the clan's treasury took its cut.

As I flipped through the pages and glanced over the information, I was stunned at how well-run this operation was. I also noticed that the dates between jobs became longer and longer, with the amount paid up front hardly covering the cost of doing the work. The clan had also stopped taking its cut. Instead, the men would get the whole amount.

Ballard made the choice to stop the deduction so his men could be better provided for. My respect for him grew the more I learned about him.

I set the book down and picked up another. This was a list of every clan member, including deaths, births, marriages, and deserters—every possible piece of information about these people that could be written down. I noticed a staggering change in the clan's numbers started fifty years ago. That must've been when the King's Guard began actively hunting them down in earnest. Women had all but stopped having children in the last fifteen years. At this rate, if nothing changed, the mercenaries as we knew them would be extinct in another forty to fifty years.

What shocked me the most was the growing number of deserters, mostly women. The clan's ratio of men to women was three to one, which certainly contributed to the lack of children being born. My bet was the women weren't willing to risk the lives of their husbands or children for a dying way of life.

I closed the book and shoved it away from me angrily. How dare they put me through all this to prove myself when their members wouldn't even think twice about abandoning the clan? I couldn't do anything for these people if they didn't want to fight for it themselves.

I glanced at the scrolls, dreading what could be written on them. I noticed one was much older, slightly yellowed, and well-worn. Gingerly, I unrolled a section and was surprised to see it was in another language.

I knew this language—not well—but better than anyone else I'd met. It was a dead language, after all. It faded out of use when our lands had been taken over generations ago. I'd learned it on a whim when I found an old text in my father's library, but Father and I didn't get a chance to work on it often with everything else my mother had me learning.

I stood up and unrolled the rest of the scroll on my bed to see if my guess was accurate. The dead language changed into our current dialect, confirming my hunch. It was a genealogy of the past royalty and dragons of this clan.

I looked around the room, trying to see if I could find some paper and a quill to write with. It would take me a little time to work out the translation, but this was one thing I knew I could do, and having a translated copy would be helpful in the future.

Walking to the desk in the corner of the room, I peeked into the first drawer, and sure enough, everything I needed was there and ready for me. I set the writing box on the desk, pulled out a quill and paring knife, and cut a new tip. I found the ink powder, mixed it with water in a small glass container, rolled the scroll to show the first three entries, and set to work.

A knock sounded at the door, but I ignored it, working on a particularly tricky section. When I didn't answer, it opened, and I looked up, surprised to see Cole standing there with a tray of food. A glance out the window showed the setting sun—apparently, I'd been working on this scroll all afternoon.

"More comfortable with books and scrolls than people, I see," Cole commented as he walked in and searched for a place to set the tray.

I scrambled, collecting the strewn papers to make space. "I guess. Studying is something I've always been good at. As you can see, it's easy for me to get lost in it."

Cole looked over my work, raising a brow. "So your father decided you learning the old tongue wouldn't sully your reputation?" Before I could answer his question, he picked up a sheet and looked over my translations. His gaze shot back to me. "Shit! You've almost translated all the entries in the old tongue! This would take most people years!"

Shrugging, I looked at the papers before me. "I love puzzles and things that challenge me. Though, being a lady, I was rarely given anything challenging to do. My father and I would have battles against each other sometimes, even if they were only on paper. He used this dialect to send messages to his army, and I intercepted them. Well, I guess in hindsight, he let me so I would learn it better." I smiled, remembering our game.

"What a strange mouse you are. Most women your age wouldn't be caught dead playing at war games," he said, not looking up from my work.

Were we actually having a conversation without one of us getting pissed at the other? I'd never seen him so relaxed. Most of the time he'd been so defensive or angry. This was a whole new side to see.

As if he noticed his change, he straightened up and cleared his throat, turning to leave. "Make sure you don't stay up too late. Morning comes early for trainees."

Apparently, we'd reached the limit of his ability to be nice. After he left the room, I rested my chin on my hand and thought over what just happened. Not only did he bring me dinner when I missed it, he'd stayed to talk. I mulled over what could have possibly happened this afternoon for him to change his attitude so much, but my thoughts were cut short by my stomach rumbling. I rolled up the scroll and collected all the papers, setting them on a shelf so they wouldn't get dirty.

"*Cass,*" Vasin called, scaring a yelp out of me.

"*Don't do that, you scared me half to death,*" I thought, exasperated.

"*Apologies, I will try not to startle you next time, but you need to get used to me doing this so it doesn't distract you.*"

"*You're right. I was just so lost in my own thoughts that it caught me off guard. Did you need me for something?*"

"*I just wanted to check on you and make sure you were feeling better.*"

"*Things went great with Ballard, just like you said. Oh, and I even started translating a scroll for the cranky historian.*"

"*I'm glad all is well.*"

"*Are you close by? It's strange to talk like this when I could talk to you face-to-face.*"

"*I'm outside your window.*"

I peered out the window, and sure enough, there he was, sitting with his tail wrapped around him like a cat.

"I will be right out!" I called aloud.

I grabbed the tray of food, jogged down the stairs, and flipped open the latch with my elbow. Helena was humming to herself as she cleaned the dinner dishes, so I tried to slip quietly past her, not wanting to bother her.

"Don't go too far from the clearing, there are dangerous animals out there," Helena called after me. "Although I guess your dragon should be able to keep you safe."

Shaking my head, I smiled as I walked out to Vasin. I should have known I wouldn't be able to sneak by Helena. Maybe someday.

"*What is the scroll about?*" Vasin asked as I settled into the fold of his front legs.

"The one I was working on is the record of the past rulers and their dragons, but I had to translate half of it," I shared, dunking my bread into the stew on my tray.

"*Did you find anything interesting about your predecessors?*"

"To be honest, I didn't really read what I was translating. I got into a rhythm, and I just went with it. I'll go back later and read it all, then I can really focus on the information."

"*Hmm. That is wise. If you need any help, I would be happy to assist you in your translation work.*"

"You can read?" Vasin's chest rumbled as he laughed at me. "How was I to know you can read? Can you write too?"

"*I have not tried to write, but I believe I might be able to... though it may be difficult without human hands. As for the reading part, I have generations of knowledge I can access, and it seems many dragons have picked up reading over the years.*"

I thought about that for a moment, and it made sense. Of course, people would want their dragons to know how to read. It was a perfect way to gather and transport information no one else could access. Having a dragon as a mercenary could make a huge difference in how information was gathered and used.

"If I get stuck, I'll have you look it over. You're quite full of surprises, my friend," I said, stifling a yawn.

"*I THINK IT WOULD BE BEST IF YOU WENT TO BED, MY DEAR CASS. YOU HAVE MANY LONG, HARD DAYS BEFORE YOU,*" Vasin said as he nuzzled me with his big head.

"Very well, I'll see you tomorrow." I scratched his eye ridges for a moment before I headed in for the night.

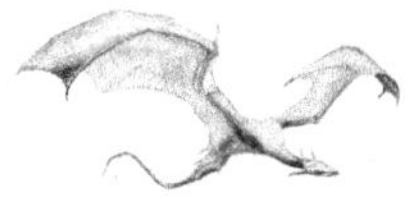

Morning came in a flash. I felt like I'd just closed my eyes when Helena was gently shaking my shoulder to wake me. When I opened my eyes, I was surprised to see it was still dark outside.

"Is there something wrong?" I croaked, not really awake.

"It's time to get ready to start training," Helena said as she lit the candles in my room.

"The sun isn't even up yet," I grumbled.

"I know this will be rough at first, but this is how all our trainees are treated, and we can't afford to change for you. I'll be back with some breakfast while you get dressed. I suggest you wear something simple and loose."

I tossed back the covers and hefted the trunk's lid back, placing one of the candles close so I could see inside. I pulled out supple leather pants, a chest wrap, and a simple white shirt. I searched for the boots I'd worn yesterday and found they'd somehow made their way under the bed. Finally dressed, I poured water into the wash bowl and scrubbed my face, washing away the last of my sleepiness with the cold water.

"Here's something simple for you. It may not look like much, but it will stick to your bones," Helena assured me as she placed the food on the table.

"I don't think I can eat right now. I never was a fan of breakfast," I said, wrinkling my nose as I looked at the bowl of lumpy mush.

"Starting now, you'll be eating breakfast every morning. I won't have you fainting from hunger later. Now eat up. Every. Last. Bite," Helena demanded, pointing at the bowl.

The stuff tasted a lot better than it looked, which was a blessing. I'm not sure I could've forced myself to eat it if it had tasted bad. Helena watched me until I finished the last bite, and I even scraped the sides of the bowl to prove I was listening.

"Good. Now come down to the kitchen. Your first teacher is waiting for you."

I sighed heavily, bracing myself for the start of this day. When I entered the kitchen, I was greeted by the sight of a towering man a few years older than me. His presence made the large room feel much smaller, and his blue eyes, which were so light they seemed gray, were trained on me. I blinked, trying not to stare more than I already had been, but it was hard when he had a body like that. His long blond hair was pulled away from his face but still hung freely past his shoulders, completing the look that would make any girl swoon.

"Lady Cassarah, I'm Abbott," he said, bowing his head to me. "I'll be your teacher for swordsmanship and hand-to-hand combat skills."

I took a heartbeat too long to respond, shocked by his decorum. "It's a pleasure to meet you, Sir Abbott. I hope to learn much from you."

Abbott smiled at me, making him even more handsome, if that was even possible. "Just Abbott. I'm no nobleman, Lady," he corrected gently.

"Oh, of course, forgive me. Call me Cassarah. I'm no longer a noble lady," I stammered, feeling flustered.

"Well then, Cassarah, shall we get started?" Abbott asked, raising an eyebrow.

"Of course. Please lead the way." I gestured for him to proceed.

I followed behind his broad back, waving farewell to Helena, who smiled and waved back. I had to jog a little to keep up with Abbott's long stride as we headed toward the forest, the sky starting to lighten into shades of purple as the sun climbed its way up.

I collided with something hard and almost fell to the ground when an arm shot out, wrapping around my waist to steady me. I'd read silly romance poems and sonnets about how the mere touch of a man could ignite feelings in a woman, and now I knew that every word was true. The heat from his arm blazed through me, causing me to shiver from a sensation I'd never experienced before.

"First lesson... you must keep your eyes focused on where you're going at all times. Someday this simple practice will keep you alive," Abbott said, letting me go.

I blushed. How could I have messed this up already? Not only did I crash into him, but now my mind was flooded with thoughts about feeling his muscular body against mine. If this was how things were starting out, I was in for a very long day.

"I understand. It won't happen again," I responded, knowing that was the answer my mother would've wanted to hear.

"Oh, it'll happen many more times, but it's best to get you to start paying attention to it from the very beginning." He winked, giving me a soft smile and setting me at ease. "Today we're just going to start with basic training and conditioning. My guess is you haven't done much physical work in your daily life."

"No, that's definitely something I was never allowed to do. Unless you count dancing lessons as physical work."

"Sadly, no. This is why we need to strengthen your body before we can even think about starting any other training. I'll show you a set of drills you'll work on every day until they become as easy as breathing. Then we can attempt to teach you some real fighting skills," Abbott explained.

We walked into an empty clearing where torches were lit, making it easy to see. I noticed a few obstacles placed around the area, and I was curious to determine why they were there.

"All right, this is the starting point." Abbott reached down and picked up a burlap sack with straps. "For now, you'll wear this rock-filled sack to speed up the strengthening process. You must never lose this sack or let any rocks spill out as you go. When this becomes too easy, I'll add more rocks, and so on.

"With this sack on your back, you'll run down this path 'til you reach the river, which you'll cross. Once on the other side, climb up the steps cut into the bluff, then find the fallen tree to get back across the river. This will lead you to the tunnel in the mountain you must crawl through. The tunnel will lead you back to the forest, where the path back is easy to figure out. Any questions?"

My mouth fell open in shock. There was no way I was going to survive this course. How did he think I could do all of that?

"I don't know how to swim." I could hear the panic rising in my voice. "How am I supposed to cross a river?"

"The first time is always the hardest, but it's also the most important. Once you do this, then you'll know you can. It gets better the next time and the time after that. All you need to do is prove to yourself that you can do it," Abbott said, putting his hands on my shoulders and squeezing them gently.

I looked up into his eyes and saw he truly felt like I could do this. I envied his ability to make it sound so simple. I wasn't kidding when I said dancing was all the exercise I'd done in many years. Did I even have the arm strength to climb up a rock wall? Small, dark places didn't bode well for me either, after being locked away in a closet as punishment.

Abbott leaned in closer, drawing my attention back to him. "I believe in you, Cassarah. Now you have to believe in yourself."

I took a shuddering breath as he helped me secure the sack of rocks to my back. The weight settled heavily on my shoulders, trying to pull me backward. I looked down the shadowed path and back at Abbott.

"I won't be too far from you, but unless you are in real trouble, I won't help you. This is all on you and your determination, but know if you come back with an empty sack, you'll do it twice tomorrow," Abbott said cheerily.

Glaring at him, I started walking down the path, not really sure I was ready to face myself head-on.

"Pick up your feet, trainee, this isn't a leisurely morning walk!" Abbott bellowed behind me, startling me into a jog. By the sound of it, a real angry Abbott was not someone I wanted to mess with.

I jogged until I ran out of breath. Stopping, I gasped for air, sweat rolling down my face and drenching my shirt. Never in my life did I think I could sweat that much just from jogging. I wiped my face with my sleeve as I trudged down the trail, walking until my breathing calmed. The sound of running water quickened my steps, thinking how wonderful cold water to drink and splash on my face sounded.

I halted as soon as I crested the hill, daunted by the sight of the river. This was no calm, gently flowing stream but a raging torrent rushing by. There was no way I could make my way across that thing. I would be carried away and drowned before I got two steps in. I walked upstream to see if there was a calmer spot for me to cross, but no such luck. Then I tried downstream with the same outcome.

Deciding I needed a moment to clear my mind, I walked over to the riverbank, dipped my hands in the freezing water, and slurped it down. It was the best water I'd ever tasted, so crisp and cool it almost made my teeth hurt. As I crouched at the water's edge, I could see something strange about how the water flowed in a particular spot. A bunch of loose boulders had found their place submerged under the water, but that wasn't the cause of what I was seeing. It was almost like something else was causing the water to crest around it.

I walked downstream until I came to the spot and found a large, thick rope staked to the riverbank. It ran just under the water's surface, unseen to the eye until you knew right where to look. I was actually going to be able to get across the river! Then I remembered how cold the water had been on my hands. I looked up to see the sun was still hidden behind the trees, unable to offer its warming rays.

I steeled myself to push through this. Abbott was right—I needed to believe I could do this. The noble lady that I'd been training to be was no longer a part of my life. This river was going to be the beginning of my cleansing.

Crouching down, I grabbed the thick, slimy rope and waded slowly into the torrent. I flinched when it hit my stomach, gasping at the stinging sensation. The water pulled at my clothes, wanting me to follow its path downstream, but I braced my feet against the boulders and pushed back.

I almost got dragged away when a branch in the water caught on the bag of rocks, pulling me off balance. My feet slid off the slippery boulders, and I went under, clinging to the rope with all my meager strength. The fear of being unable to breathe with the icy chill that locked me in place sent my heart racing. The burn of my lungs and the water pressing in on me gave me the push I needed to find my footing again, driving my head above water, gulping in air. Coughing, trying to learn how to breathe again, and shaking my wet hair out of my face, I forced myself to keep going.

I pulled myself the rest of the way across the river, my hands numb and fumbling. Adrenaline still coursing through my body, I somehow managed to climb up the embankment. I sprawled out on my back, breathing heavily, when I started to giggle. The giggles turned into a hysterical laugh and then into sobs.

How had I ended up in this situation? What fate had I been born into that I ended up soaking wet, laying on a muddy riverbank with a sack of rocks strapped to my back?

After I pulled myself together, I wiped my face with a partially clean part of my sleeve and stood up. I felt like a drowned rat. I looked down at my mud-covered clothes and wondered what my mother would think of me now. I tried to scrape some off but quickly gave up when all I accomplished was grinding the mud deeper into my shirt.

I searched the bluff before me to find the steps Abbott told me would be there, yet I saw nothing but vertical rock. I walked upstream a few steps, peering at the rock, then found a place that had smooth holes cut into it. They looked like they'd been etched out by people using them to climb to the top. I wouldn't have called them steps by any stretch of the imagination, but I was beginning to see this course was meant to be more of a personal challenge.

The bag of rocks on my back somehow seemed much heavier now that it was wet, making scaling the bluff even harder. My boots slipped on the crumbling rock, almost sending me crashing into the ground. Thankfully, I wasn't high enough to kill myself if I fell.

What seemed like hours later, I reached the top without incident. My hands, now covered in cuts and scrapes from the rocks, ached. I blew on them to try and get them to stop stinging, but it didn't help much. Looking around, I found a trail to follow, which led me to the fallen tree I was supposed to cross over. I peered over the edge of the bluff. Here, it was three times as high as the distance I'd just climbed. If I fell, I might not survive. How comforting.

The tree was old and had crumbled in some areas, but it looked decent enough to cross. I placed one foot gingerly on the trunk, testing it for weak spots, but it was solid under my weight. I stood for a moment to get my balance and looked straight ahead, imagining this was one of my mother's decorum lessons. Pretending I had a book on my head and needed to keep it there, I kept my shoulders back, eyes forward, and feet light but steady. I could hear my teacher scolding me to keep my chin up because "the ground will always be there, so no need to look at it." Before I knew it, my foot hit air, and I toppled off the tree and onto the grass on the other side.

Popping up off the ground, I yelled, feeling pride swell up in my chest. "Take that, Mother! See if you could walk so perfectly across a tree over a raging river of death!"

I spun around and jogged down the path with renewed strength to find the next part of my course. The path dead-ended at a towering stone wall where I was supposed to find the tunnel I was to maneuver through. It was hidden by a group of bushes on either side, the entrance wide enough for a full-grown man to fit in hunched close to the ground. Just as I feared, the tunnel was pitch black. Just looking at it caused my panic to rise.

Memories of my mother locking me in a small cupboard in my room burst to the surface. I gulped, shaking, trying to slow my breathing so I wouldn't pass out. This part I wasn't sure I could face on my own.

Some things couldn't be conquered by forcing yourself to do it, and some would never be fixed. Being here was so freeing that I'd almost started to believe I might be able to forget the horrible things my mother had done to me as a child.

Thirteen

MEMORIES

I don't know how long I sat there staring at the opening, tears streaming down my cheeks as I was assaulted with memories. Vaguely, I heard someone walking up to me.

"Cassarah, what's wrong? Did you hurt yourself?" Abbott asked, his voice freeing me from my nightmares.

Closing my eyes, I took a deep breath and said, "I can't go in there."

My muscles tightened, ready for my punishment for not following orders, but nothing came. Opening my eyes, I found Abbott sitting cross-legged in front of me, waiting with sadness in his eyes. Slowly, he leaned forward and reached out toward me, and just before he grabbed my hand, he paused so I could pull away if I wanted to. When I didn't, he took my hand in his large, rough one and squeezed it.

"What bothers you more, the darkness or the small space?"

Pulling my hand back, I cocked my head to the side, looking at the tunnel in question. "Both. When I was younger and did something my mother deemed 'unladylike,' she'd lock me in a small cupboard in my room for hours on end, even as long as a day. She never told me when she was going to let me out, and sometimes I wondered if she would." I paused, taking a shuddering breath.

It was then I realized this was the first time I had ever talked about this with someone other than Becka. *What must he think of me? Would he understand anything I was saying?*

I looked back at Abbott, expecting to see his face filled with pity or horror. I wasn't ready for the look of pure fury that glittered in his eyes. Abbott may come off as a gentle giant, but that look told me he was anything but. He finally noticed I was watching him and schooled his face, but having seen his anger, I could still notice it lurking.

His outrage for me compelled me to be honest about why I didn't feel I could ever overcome my fears. "When I got older, she started beating me, and when that still didn't get the result she wanted, she started beating Becka. So I stopped fighting, unwilling to let my only friend take the abuse I brought on myself for what I lacked. I gave up because I'm a weak, useless noblewoman who is only worthy of being married off to some stranger."

"You are not weak," Abbott snapped. "What you did wasn't weakness. You did what it took to survive, to protect Becka. Only a strong person could have made that choice."

"She shouldn't have needed to be protected. It was my fault in the first place. I was arrogant and didn't know my place in life."

"Bullshit. Your place is wherever the hell you want it to be."

"That's what I used to think when I was younger."

"It's about time we get you thinking that way again. That is what all this is about. Sure, being trained and earning the respect of the people is part of it, but you have no clue how strong you are."

"Yes, I'm so strong." I sniffled, rolling my eyes. "I can't even look at that tunnel without being frozen in fear."

"Because you're looking at it all wrong. Changing your mindset is going to be a bigger battle in all this than changing your body. You have to make the choice that you're not going to be trapped by your mother anymore. That you're going to fight for yourself and your freedom."

"You make it sound so easy. I've had fifteen years of that being beaten out of me."

Abbott shook his head, huffing at me. "That's what you're not getting. Your fight's not gone. You have it locked so deep inside you can't see it. I watched you the whole time, and believe me when I say you've got fire in your soul bursting to come out."

Who was this woman Abbott was talking about? There was no way it could be me. Fire in my soul? Right. More like ashes from where the fire's been smothered.

"I'm going to tell you the layout of the tunnel and see if that helps. It goes straight for twenty paces or so before it declines slightly, then it becomes much steeper where you'll end up sliding the rest of the way down. It's a short drop but one that comes up quickly. Once you're at the bottom, it's another ten paces to the exit."

I started to open my mouth to tell him there was no way, but he stopped me. "You're not trapped... there is a way in and a way out. No one is keeping you there. You can go as fast or slow as you like, and I will be waiting for you on the other side."

He was right. This was my choice. I was deciding to enter a dark, small place. I wasn't being forced to so I could walk away at any time. Looking into Abbott's eyes one last time, I moved toward the tunnel. Repeating the truth as a mantra, I hunched over and waddled through the entrance, bracing myself on the tunnel walls.

Let's see if this fire can be reborn.

Farther into the tunnel, I thought about crawling on my hands and knees, but when I felt the ground, it was covered in loose rock.

Not wanting to end up with bloody knees as well as hands, I decided against it. Slowly, I worked my way down the tunnel, counting my steps until the ground began to shift downward. Just like he said, it happened slowly at first, then my feet began to slide on the loose rocks as it became steeper. A rock shot out from under my foot, sending me careening down the incline. I screamed as I tumbled down the dark tunnel, fear clawing at me. Finally, I landed in a heap after being shot out and dropped into the other dark part of the tunnel.

I willed my eyes to see something, anything, terror rising in me at the thought of being trapped. Then I saw a faint, soft glow of light to my left. I crawled toward it, not caring about the rocks cutting into my skin. When I emerged from the tunnel, the sun was bright and blinding.

I'd survived!

I noticed that I felt a little lighter and pulled the sack off. A rock must have cut into the sack, and it was now all but empty. Perfect, just perfect. Hopefully, he'd been kidding that I would have to do this twice tomorrow.

"I told you that you would finish it," Abbott said, grinning from ear to ear as he held out a hand and pulled me to my feet. "Now, let's finish the course together."

As we rounded a corner of trees, I stopped in my tracks. The once-open path was now blocked by fallen trees stacked in varying heights. Abbott took off at a brisk jog, easily making his way over the blockades. I should've known it wouldn't be that easy for me. Five walls later, I was on the open path once again. I tried my best to jog my way back, but I was exhausted and decided for a steady, trudging pace that would get me back alive and breathing. When I made it to the clearing, I collapsed onto the soft grass, panting. Even without the added weight of the rocks, the last part had been hell.

Abbott sat beside me as I rolled over, looking up at him. "Here, have some water. Helena also brought us some lunch."

I sat up and gulped down the water, letting it spill out of my mouth and down my face, feeling its coolness refresh me.

"That is one hell of a course, Abbott," I said, wiping off the water on my chin. "I'm amazed I survived it. How do you keep from losing some of your new trainees on this trail?"

"In the spirit of sharing, I want to be honest with you." Abbott hesitated at the frown I felt growing on my face. "This course is for trainees to test their endurance and see if they can move up to advanced training."

I felt my jaw fall open as I stared at him in disbelief. "Are you kidding me?! You made me go through all that unprepared?"

"I told you there was a fire inside you, and now you can't deny it. No one weak of mind or spirit could have managed to pull that off."

I thought about what he said for a moment. If I hadn't been forced into making myself do this, I would've never thought I could. He was trying to make me believe I was stronger than I thought, and in a way, he'd been right. I'd just accomplished something I never would have attempted had I known.

"I understand why you did it, but if I find out you did this to me again, I'm not sure I'll ever be able to trust you," I said, locking eyes with him.

"I understand," Abbott answered as he tucked a wayward curl behind my ear. "From now on, I promise I'll be upfront and honest about my intentions. That being said, now that I've seen what you're capable of, I'm holding you to that standard. Many trainees give up once they cross the river, but you didn't. You even pushed yourself through a panic attack." Abbott grinned, respect showing in his eyes.

"I have no doubt you could be the best trainee we've seen in a long time."

"Thank you, Abbott, for helping me do this." I sighed. "Although I did lose the rocks out of my sack."

"Well, I guess tomorrow you'll have to do it twice."

I slumped at the response. "Kill me now."

"Don't worry about that now. Rest and eat your lunch. It will all be easier in time."

Helena had packed us a lunch of cured meat, cheese, and bread with some apples. I couldn't believe how hungry I was after that workout. I didn't worry about taking dainty, ladylike bites—I tore off chunks and shoved them in my mouth. Abbott chuckled at me, but I didn't feel that awkward since he was eating the same way, albeit slower than I was.

"Did you grow up here?" I asked.

"Yes, but I was actually born into one of the other clans. When my parents died, my clan brought me to Ballard, and he took me in and raised me alongside Cole."

I wanted to smack myself for bringing up the subject when Ballard had told me this yesterday. Now here I was, forcing him to talk about his parents' death. Good going, Cass.

"I'm so sorry about your parents. That's awful."

"You'd be surprised at how often it happens in this way of life. Many go on a job and come back safe, but there is always the chance you might never return."

"Is that why people have been leaving?" I questioned, remembering my reading from last night.

Abbott shrugged. "I guess that could be part of it. Personally, I think it has more to do with having to live in secret. We didn't always have to hide in the woods like thieves. We used to work with Norden, but something happened, and they turned on us. No one to this day knows what occurred."

"Last night I was working on translating one of the older scrolls. Maybe it's written down but just lost to us right now."

Abbott's eyes widened in surprise. "You can read our original tongue?"

"I might not be so good in the physical arena, but I'm very skilled in the brains department." I smiled, loving the reaction I was getting from him. "My father made sure I learned many things a normal noble lady wouldn't. I'm quite the strategist if I do say so myself."

It was nice to finally show what I could do well instead of focusing on where I fell short.

"Hmm, we'll have to set you up against Ballard and see who's the better strategist. He's scary in how he thinks of trapping people in their own plans. It's a sight to see," Abbott said, his eyes flashing with excitement.

"I'll have to bring that up to him later," I said, smiling back.

"Wait 'til we get you trained in fighting, then you'll be near unstoppable. You'll have beauty, brains, and brawn," Abbott said, a glint of something in his eyes I'd never seen directed at me before.

Fourteen

Training

After lunch with Abbott, I went to the stable to meet with the person training me on riding. Much to my surprise, I was greeted with a much-needed familiar face.

"Becka! When did you get here?" I said, rushing to hug her.

"Last night." Becka laughed, hugging me back. "I'm glad to see you well, m'lady."

"None of that." I frowned at her, knowing she was teasing me. Still, I was so glad to have her here for this, to finally have someone who understood what I came from.

Becka smiled at my silliness. "Come on, let's get your lesson started."

"You're teaching me how to ride?"

"I happen to be the daughter of the clan's stablemaster. I was riding horses long before I could walk. Not even my old man can best me at trick riding," Becka said, her blue eyes shining with pride.

"How have I known you my whole life but know practically nothing about you?" I asked. I hung my head, unable to look her in the face.

"It was part of my job to keep an eye on your family, so even if you'd asked, I wouldn't have told you the truth. Your family is the only one that has ever left the clan to gain riches that were not earned, so the clan always had a presence in their home to make sure they didn't sell out the rest of us," Becka explained, taking my hand in hers and squeezing it gently. "Come on, the lesson will take your mind off past things. You have a new future to live for now."

"I guess the bright side is that we've been riding a bunch of times, so you already know what you're working with." I smiled, remembering picnics out in the fields with my father and Becka before Mother would deem we'd been gone long enough and send a manservant for us. "I think Father would've loved living among these people. They are so like-minded."

"It would make sense since this is your lineage. Quick wit runs thick in this bunch," Becka commented, grinning.

"So where do you want to start?" I asked once we reached Grace's stall.

"We'll start where everyone should... the beginning," Becka said, handing me a brush. "Get her all brushed out, and then we'll go over saddling her up. Depending on how fast you pick that up, we might get you in the saddle today."

"Funny, Becka, really funny," I said, opening Grace's door, grabbing her halter, and tying her to the stall door.

True to her word, we went over all the basics of taking care of a horse for the next hour. Then we moved onto learning all the parts of the saddle and bridle before I could even put it on.

"Why are there so many things to know about such a simple saddle?" I grumbled as I was *finally* allowed to put it on the horse.

"Knowledge is power. It could be the difference between making it out of a situation or not. Think of it this way... you're in a fight and someone manages to cut up your saddle. If you know every inch of it, you'll know whether it's safe to keep using or if you need to ditch it before you get hurt."

With Grace now finally saddled under Becka's watchful eye, we moved on to the arena.

"We will now be attempting to get you on your horse." Becka grinned at me like a cat who'd just caught a mouse.

"Finally. So, are you going to help me up, or do you have a mounting block for me to use?" I questioned, looking around the arena since I knew the saddle had no stirrups.

Becka just looked at me, shaking her head. "No, Cassarah, you're going to learn how to get in the saddle without any help. As I explained, having stirrups on the saddle adds something you could get hung up on in trick riding. You need to know how to get on your horse without anything to aid you."

Now her evil grin from earlier made more sense. She knew I was never going to get on Grace today. Either that, or she was expecting miracles to happen.

"Don't give me that look. Here, let me show you," Becka said as she walked up to Grace's shoulder. "Now grab some of her mane here at the base of her neck, then take a step away, then hop forward and swing right on up."

Becka made the whole action look so effortless, like simply leaping onto a horse was no big deal. Sadly, I'd never had any reason to leap in my life until now.

I steeled myself and squared my shoulders. I could do this. I walked up to Grace and positioned myself like I'd seen Becka do a moment ago. Becka was close by, watching everything I was doing, giving me pointers as I prepared.

"Grasp her mane tightly. You won't hurt her. Now the trick to this is not to doubt yourself. If you do, then you'll never make it in the saddle. Just take your step back and go for it. No second-guessing."

I took a deep breath and pictured myself going through the motions and landing smoothly in the saddle. I opened my eyes, took a step back, and leaped with all the effort I had. For a moment, I thought I had it and was going to do this on my first try. I could see my leg making its way almost over the saddle just before I slammed into Grace's side and fell to the ground.

"That was amazing, Cassarah! You should be very proud of yourself," Becka exclaimed, offering me a hand up with a wide grin. "No one ever makes it on the first try, and most people don't actually get their feet off the ground."

"I have a feeling I'm going to be used to falling off a horse by the time I figure this out," I grumbled, brushing off my bruised rump.

Becka chuckled. "I never thought of it that way, but it's actually a good thing to get used to. Saves you worrying about it later. Now dust yourself off and try again."

After five more tries, Grace started to get upset with me and would move just as I was getting ready to throw myself at her. A moving target was ten times harder to even *try* to swing myself up on. Crashing to the ground yet again, I laid there, looking up at the wooden beams of the arena's ceiling.

"I can't feel my butt anymore," I whined as Becka came to loom over me.

"Your ass is big enough to handle it," she teased, making me gape at her. "Let's call it a day. Even the world's most patient horse can't take much more of this."

Rolling over, I groaned as I got to my feet. Muscles I didn't even know I had were crying out at the abuse. "Thank God. I don't know how much longer I could have kept that up."

"Get Grace settled for the night, then you can head back to the house. Helena should be waiting with dinner for you. Let's do this again tomorrow," Becka said, waving and heading out of the arena.

Getting Grace set for the night took more effort than I thought it would. My arms felt like noodles, unwilling to be held up for any length of time. Finally brushed, watered, and fed, Grace was good until the next day. Slowly, I trudged back to the house and climbed the few steps before flopping down at the large kitchen table.

"Goodness, child, you look like you got trampled," Helena tutted as she set a bowl of stew and a plate of bread in front of me.

"I'm glad I look like I feel," I mumbled, dipping bread into the bowl.

After doing that a few times, I gave up and picked the bowl up with both hands and poured it into my mouth. I didn't care what I looked like. I was starving and didn't have the energy to do much more. Setting down the bowl, I looked up to find the rest of the table watching me with wide eyes. Abbott even had his spoon frozen halfway to his mouth while Cole tried not to laugh.

Helena glared at him before she looked over at me. "I'm thinking you need seconds but not sure you'll stay awake for it. Come on, let's get you cleaned up and to bed."

She took my dishes to the sink and came back to assist me up the stairs to my room. I fell back on the bed while Helena helped get my boots off. Done with that, she left and returned with a small tub, followed by Cole who had two buckets of hot water. He poured them in and quickly left, not saying a word.

"Let's get a move on, child. You'll not be filling your sheets with half the sand from the arena. Chop, chop." Helena clapped, giving me the motivation to get up.

I sank into the scalding water and felt my muscles sigh with relief as they relaxed. I scrubbed my scalp to make sure all the sand packed in there was truly gone. Out of the tub, Helena dried me off briskly and sat me down in the chair, setting on my hair with a comb. I must have fallen asleep at some point because the next thing I knew, I was being shaken to get in bed.

"Poor thing, these next few weeks are going to be tough on you," Helena murmured as she pulled the blankets up around me. "Sleep well."

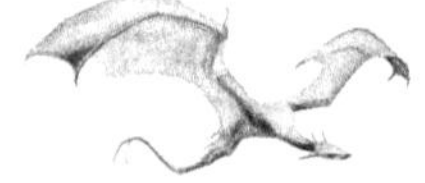

The next morning went much the same—up before the sun, eating breakfast, and meeting up with Abbott. True to his word, I had to do the course twice, but this time it didn't take me nearly as long to accomplish. I still struggled with the tunnel, but the repetition helped to ease some of the panic.

Since I finished faster, Abbott and I worked on some sword skills. He handed me a weighted pole, showed me some basic stances, and had me repeat each drill twenty times before moving on. Even with the cool fall breeze, I was dripping in sweat, my shirt clinging to me as I laid in the grass, catching my breath.

"You're catching on quickly, Cassarah. You should be proud of yourself," Abbott said, handing me a jug of water.

I sat up to grab it, and our fingers overlapped as I took the water from him. Trying to hide my blush, I gulped the water down, relishing the coolness of it. "If I can use my arms for anything else today, then I'll be proud. I thought they hurt yesterday, but I was mistaken."

Abbott laughed as he unpacked the lunch Helena sent with us. "Once you get past the pain and soreness, it gets better. I remember my training days. I was ten when I first started. Believe it or not, I was always a chubby kid and wasn't very skilled at anything, but it made me work harder, seeing everyone else advancing faster than I was. Now I'm the best swordsman in our clan and not too shabby with my fists, either."

Taking in Abbott's muscular body, it was hard to picture him as a chubby, unsure kid. The godlike physique and graceful confidence with his skills in swordsmanship would make any woman—me included—swoon. I understood his point, though, and I knew I needed to keep pushing myself if I were going to manage all this in a year.

"Seems someone is ready to start the next lesson," Abbott muttered, looking over my shoulder.

I turned to see Cole walking over to us with a very determined look on his face. Getting to my feet, I dusted off the grass and leaves from my pants and took a deep breath, readying myself for what was coming next.

"Don't brush yourself off too much. I have a feeling you'll end up on the ground quite a bit more in our lesson," Cole sneered once he reached us.

"Wonderful," I groaned, looking beseechingly at Abbott.

"See you at dinner," Abbott said, giving me a sympathetic smile as he left.

"First, we're going to work on strength training. I can only imagine how weak your muscles must be after all that needlepoint," Cole said, looking me over with a furrowed brow and arms crossed.

"I'll have you know I'm stronger than I look." I huffed, irritated he assumed I was some wilting flower, even if I kind of was.

"We'll see about that. Follow me… we're heading to the arena." With that, Cole spun on his heel without looking back.

Dashing after him as he took off, we walked through the barn and into the attached arena. It seemed a shipment of supplies had been brought in and stacked on one end.

"See those bags of horse feed?" Cole pointed to a pile of twenty-five burlap sacks that were half my size. "I want you to move them to the other end of the arena. When you're done with that, you'll climb that rope and ring the bell at the top. Once those things are complete, we will do some drills for hand-to-hand combat."

My mouth fell open. I was already exhausted from the training this morning. How was I going to be able to do all that without dying? And I still had to read the rest of the books Sal gave me so I could go over them with him tomorrow.

"Feel free to start whenever you're ready," Cole commented, pulling out a book and making himself comfortable on a haybale. "We won't be leaving until you complete everything, so take as long as you like."

I clenched my fists and marched over to the pile of feed sacks, determined to wipe the smugness from his tone. I bear-hugged the first one and managed to get it off the stack, but it slid out of my arms to the ground when I stood. I squatted and tried to heave the bag up, but I couldn't keep my grip on it. So I grabbed the two top corners and started to drag it. With this method, I managed to easily get five bags to the other side. With each sack, I could feel my arms screaming, my hands cramping, and my lower back complaining at the demand.

"Only twenty more to go, little mouse," Cole called from the sidelines.

"Contrary to your belief, I know how to count. I'm well aware of how many more I have to move," I snapped.

Cole harrumphed and went back to his book.

I lost track of time as I focused on getting this task done. I wouldn't give him the satisfaction of seeing me fail miserably as he expected. I knew it was no longer light outside because Cole went around and lit the lanterns so he could keep reading his book. Sweat stung my eyes as it rolled off my brow, my sleeves covered in grime from using them to wipe my face.

Only seven more to go before I was finished, and I would be damned if I left this undone. My anger and irritation at Cole fueled my body, keeping it in motion. If not for him sitting there without a care in the world, I would have given up long ago.

Twenty-three done, two more to go. My hands were so cramped I couldn't hold onto the sack—it just kept slipping out of my grasp. I bear-hugged it this time and tried to hoist it up on my shoulder. Doing so, I knocked myself over, falling backward with the grain sack landing on top of me. I groaned in pain, and my body cried out at the abuse I was putting it through. I laid there a second, trying to catch my breath and figure out how I was going to get these last two sacks to the other side.

Cole's face loomed over mine, his brow surprisingly furrowed in worry. "Cassarah, are you okay? Here, let me get this off you."

"Don't you lay one damn finger on me or the feed sack," I growled. "I will finish this *without* your assistance. Now. Back. Off."

He really didn't believe I could do this on my own. At the first sign I was in trouble or hurt, he came running. I bet he wouldn't have come to my rescue if I'd been any other trainee.

I rolled the feed sack off my chest and managed to sit up. Cole didn't try to reach out and help but stepped away, arms crossed over his chest. I heaved myself to my feet, grasped the sack, and pulled with all my strength. Making it to the other side, I flopped down on top of the stack, taking a few deep breaths. Dragging myself up, I went back for the final sack, my body screaming at me to stop and rest. I didn't know if I had any strength left to move that last sack, let alone keep standing.

I would figure out something, though. I was so close to finishing this.

My legs gave out when I reached for the last sack, dropping me to my knees. I placed my head on the sack, searching deep within to find any last ounce of energy. Finding none, I felt a hopelessness crashing down on me.

Suddenly, a warmth flowed through me, easing some of the pain and bringing life back into tired muscles.

"Cass, you still don't understand... I am always with you. Let me lend you some of my strength, and we will finish this together. Your determination is inspiring, but together we are even more powerful."

Vasin's soothing voice flowed through my body, reviving my lost endurance and then some. I opened myself up to let Vasin's healing balm course through my body, reassured by the fact I had someone who always believed in me.

I grasped the last sack and tossed it over my shoulder like it was featherlight, then walked the final time across the arena. I tossed it with the others and looked at the pile proudly.

"Thank you for always encouraging me, Vasin. I don't think I'd be able to survive this without you."

I could feel Vasin's pleasure at my words as his warmth left me as did the second wind he brought. I plopped to the ground, happy and exhausted beyond words.

After a few moments collecting myself, I lurched to my feet and stumbled over to the climbing rope, grabbing it with both hands. Not surprisingly, my arms gave out when I tried to pull myself up, and I collapsed to the ground. I glared up at the rope as if it was its fault I couldn't make it to the top.

"What do you think you're doing?" Cole demanded, walking over to me.

"You said I couldn't be done 'til I climbed the rope and then did the drills," I mumbled, not looking at him.

"That was never going to happen, you idiot. I didn't even think you'd be able to move all the feed across the arena." Cole sighed, reaching a hand out to me. "Come on, let's head back home and get some food in you before you pass out."

Pissed, I slapped his hand away. "You did all this to see me give up?"

All my life I'd had people using me as they saw fit, treating me like I was there for their personal amusement. I know I didn't have much belief in myself through all this, but for him to purposely design this to make me fail was going too far. I felt tears pricking the corners of my eyes, and my chest tightened with the effort to stop them. Just like my mother, I knew I couldn't show Cole my tears, but I was past the point of being able to control them.

Cole kneeled so that we were at eye level. "Don't cry. Anything but that, please."

"Why do you hate me so much?" I asked, feeling a tear escape and roll down my cheek. "What did I do that was so wrong for you to treat me like you do? I'm the one who gave up everything to come here. Now I have to try and prove I'm worthy to an entire clan of people who don't want me. I know I'm not good enough... no one else needs to tell me that."

Cole hung his head, and his shoulders slumped forward. "Look, I don't hate you. I hate where you come from. My parents were killed on a job, attacked by Lord Everett's men when I was little. My grandparents were the ones who raised me. When I look at you, all I see is your social status and title. Your kind took my family from me because nobles think they are so superior and we are disposable."

He looked up at me then, and for the first time, I felt like I was really seeing the true Cole. I knew what it was like to keep your true self hidden to keep your pain locked inside. I was beginning to figure out that the arrogant Cole was the face of someone wounded by loss. He was so filled with anger and vengeance for his family that he had no room for kindness.

"I'm sorry I've been such an asshole to you. Even though I have my issues with nobles, it doesn't mean you're like that. It's just that letting someone have power over the only family I've got left scares the fuck out of me. I wanted to hate you so it would be easier to get rid of you," Cole admitted. "Thing is, I've been impressed with you since I snuck onto your balcony that first night. I've never had a woman willing to put an arrow through me for hitting on her. It was kind of hot."

Unable to control myself, I burst into laughter. Of all the things I thought Cole would say to me, that wasn't it. I laughed so hard tears started to seep out of my eyes.

"You shocked the hell out of me today," Cole said once I stopped laughing. "Abbott told me how well you did on the obstacle course yesterday. I thought it was just dumb luck... no way could a prissy noble lady be turned into a mercenary. It just doesn't happen. I needed you to prove yourself to me and know what your breaking point was. If I was going to be asked to risk my life for you as our queen and leader, then I needed to know the type of person you really are. Time and time again, you've shown me something different than I assumed," Cole said, standing and reaching out a hand to help me up. "I guess it took me until now to see you might be more stubborn than anyone I've ever met."

"So does this mean we can work on being at least civil to each other?" I asked, looking from his hand to his face, not wanting to fall for some prank.

"Yeah, sure, whatever. But understand this changes nothing about how I train you."

I grasped his hand and let him pull me up. "I would expect nothing less."

Fifteen

History

"Sal, you here?" I called, seeing the desk he usually sat at was empty.

Hearing rustling from the sea of bookshelves off to my left, I wandered in that direction, maneuvering around piles of books and scrolls stacked randomly in the aisles. The wealth of information that could be found in this place amazed me.

Over the past five months, Sal and I had decided to find as many old books I could help translate as possible. Numerous items had been lost in attacks on the clan throughout the years, but with the vast memory of the recordkeeper, some were recreated. I was getting much more proficient at my translations now that I was doing it every day, and I was even teaching it to Sal and his apprentice, Isabell, so we could get more done.

"Cassy, that you?"

I cringed at the nickname he insisted on using. "Yeah, Sal, where are you?"

"Over in the section of the Great War."

Figured. Sal had me working on translating those records since it was a time in our history we didn't have a lot of information on. The Great War happened two hundred years ago between Norden and all the mercenary clans, and it was the beginning of our demise. There were five major mercenary clans in our land, and before the Great War, they worked together under the mercenary king or queen to keep the kingdom running smoothly alongside the capital's royalty.

As I translated each text, I was helping to uncover more information about the history of not only our clan, but the others, each of which had its own traditions and were represented by a different colored dragon. The black dragon had always signified the Raven Rose clan. The Jade Talon clan had the green dragon, the Hell Hawk clan the red dragon, the Bronze Reaper clan the brown dragon, and the Wind Fists clan the blue dragon. Apparently, the golden female had always paired with a royal from the capital, and the purple dragon seemed to come and go in our history. Most of the other mercenary clans were now on the verge of extinction due to Lord Everett's plans to finish what Norden started so many years ago. It was becoming clear my biggest task in ruling these people would be to find a way to help those clans regain their past prosperity.

When I finally found Sal, he was surrounded by open books strewn haphazardly around him, ink stains all over his hands and sleeves.

"Um, everything okay?" I asked.

"I'm close! I finally found records from the time of the Raven Queen. During her rule, the clans prospered like none before. She was also one of the only queens to take all her guardians as lovers and marry them," Sal gushed, his wrinkled face glowing with excitement. "This book is an advisor's personal account of his time with the queen, but he only ever addresses her by her title, not her given name."

Squatting near him, I took the book he held out and skimmed over the passage. "This definitely sounds like the woman I've been dreaming about. Oh, look... here it even talks about her dragon, Cheery."

Sal snagged the book out of my hands and looked to where I pointed. "Thank the dragons, we're finally getting somewhere."

"You do realize we've translated more than any other generation has before us. I would say we are more than getting somewhere."

"Yes, yes, but this is information that has been truly lost to us. We don't have much on her daughter, Queen Emery, because of the Great War. So many records were destroyed, and nothing was written for fear it would fall into the wrong hands. To this day, we still don't really know what happened to cause the divide between us and the monarchy. If you truly want to build us back to our former glory, that knowledge is going to be invaluable. Now take this stack with you to work on next," Sal said, waving at six books he'd stashed off to the side.

Collecting my books, I left Sal's house, knowing I wasn't going to get anything helpful from Sal while he was like this. Once he latched onto something, he wouldn't be deterred until he found what he was looking for. With that in mind, I headed back home to start work on the books in my arms.

My life had fallen into a new rhythm of early mornings and late nights. I would have five days of various combat training, then I would spend a day with Sal learning about my role and translating. Thankfully, I got a day off once a week to do as I pleased. Most of those days, Vasin and I would go flying, getting to know the mountains we now called home. We would also spend those days working on things only he could teach me, like how to use my Birthright and how to strengthen our connection over distances.

The stronger I grew in our connection, the more often I had dreams of the past. It seemed I was following the life of one of our past queens—the Raven Queen, as the historical texts called her. Some nights I felt like I was intruding as I watched her falling in love with her guardians and them with her. Then other times I watched her as a child with her loving parents. It got to the point I felt like I knew her as well as I knew myself. I still couldn't figure out why this particular ancestor had decided to latch on to me.

"Cassarah, Earth to Cassarah," Becka's voice finally broke through my thoughts.

"Becka?" I startled, looking up from a scroll I was supposed to be reading. "Sorry, lost in thought and didn't hear you come in."

"I was asking if you wanted to join some of us on a hunt tomorrow. It would be a great chance for you to test out your skills. You're doing great learning all the riding tricks, but that's in an arena. We need to get you out into the real world," Becka said, her eyes alight with excitement.

"Does that mean I can skip the normal training? I'm happy to go if that's the case," I said, grinning. "I won't get better without a real-life situation to challenge me, after all."

With Abbott and Cole training me, I was getting stronger and faster every day, but I still had much to learn. Abbott beat sword drills into me until I did them perfectly, even in my sleep. He even added a heavy, weighted leather vest and bracers for me to wear when we fought hand-to-hand. As for my work with Cole, I was now a master rope climber, feed-sack tosser, and well on my way to getting myself out of any knife fight. He said we would soon be moving on to live steel instead of wooden daggers for our sessions. I could also pick a lock faster than anyone in the clan.

"Perfect. I'll let everyone know you're going. The boys will be happy too, since now they can come with. I'll let you get back to studying."

Becka paused at the door and turned to look back at me. "You really should be proud of yourself... you're doing amazing."

"Thanks, Becka," I said, smiling at her as she waved goodbye and left me to my studies.

Lost once more in my reading, I smiled, feeling the fire of determination growing. Just like Abbott promised, I'd been able to revive the passion and confidence my mother had smothered. Through our time training together, Abbott had become a steady constant in my life. He pushed me further than I thought I could go, but he was always there to pick me up when I fell. The soothing way he helped me work through my fears and conquer them drew us closer.

Cole had also become someone I leaned on, though he was the opposite of Abbott's calm. Cole was the spark to light the tinder in my spirit. He got under my skin and brought out my competitive side. Everything between us started as a clash, driving me to prove him wrong, and even though most of our conversations still ended in an argument, I knew he had my back.

A tapping on my connection to Vasin interrupted my thoughts. "*Cass, come take a break from the past. A lesson outside in the fresh air will do you good. Your nose has been buried in books all day.*"

"*A break sounds good. I was getting a bit stiff sitting here. Hey, how far back does your memory go?*"

"*I have memories from the very first dragon hatched here and bound to a human. It seems that any time before we paired ourselves to your kind has been lost. In my opinion, the fact we started bonding with humans created the chain of memories.*"

"*I have to admit, that is one amazing ability you guys have,*" I mused out loud as I headed down to the kitchen.

I plucked an apple out of the bowl on the table, waving at Helena as I left out the back door.

"Don't go too far. Dinner will be ready in an hour!" Helena called after me.

"Okay," I said over my shoulder.

"THERE IS NO NEED FOR US TO GO VERY FAR. WE CAN PRACTICE IN THE WOODS NEARBY," Vasin said as I reached him.

It was crazy to me to see how much he'd grown before my eyes over the past months. He was now as big and stocky, far larger than a draft horse, and his wingspan was so large we needed to take off in the meadows. I reached up to scratch his head, now the same size as my torso.

"What did you have in mind for today?" I asked as we ambled our way to the forest behind the house.

"NOW THAT YOU CAN REACH ME ACROSS LONG DISTANCES AND DON'T HAVE TO RELY ON YOUR EMOTIONS TO TRIGGER YOUR BIRTHRIGHT, I WANT TO WORK ON HARMONIZING. I HAVE BEEN WARY OF EXPOSING YOU TO THAT CONNECTION BECAUSE OF WHAT HAPPENED WHEN YOU VENTURED TOO FAR INTO MY CON-SCIOUSNESS. I DO NOT THINK THESE DREAMS ARE HARMFUL TO YOU, BUT I STILL DO NOT UNDERSTAND WHY THEY UNLOCKED IN YOU AS THEY WOULD FOR US DRAGONS," Vasin explained, watching me out of the corner of his eye.

I looked down at my hands as I thought of the incident he was talking about. When I'd reached out to him, I'd found a presence in his consciousness. I chased after it, almost causing me to be lost in his memories forever. Now looking back on it, I believe that presence was Miranda, whose memories I'd been seeing in my dreams.

"I trust you to know if I'm ready to try and explore that again. Now that I know what I'm getting into, I think I can handle things better," I reassured him, taking a deep breath.

"I must confess, when you told me of the figure, it made me curious as to why you can see this apparition. I have searched through all my memories and have been unable to find anything related to this."

"What I find strange is I've been watching her life over the past six months."

"Come. Hopefully, we will discover this presence again, and we can investigate it."

I settled against Vasin's chest and took a deep breath, closing my eyes. I reached out to Vasin, and this time, instead of opening myself to him, I melded with his consciousness. When I felt the connection solidify, I opened my eyes to see the world as he did. Everything was sharper, from the color to the amount of detail. It was like I could almost see each tiny vein in a leaf twenty feet away. I could feel the heat of his ember deep in his chest, which had been growing in strength but not yet strong enough to breathe fire. I could feel my body's warmth against his cold scales, but I could also sense that my body was void of something.

"This is why I always say we must never harmonize if you're in danger. Your body's left vulnerable to any kind of attack. Of course, you are safe now because I am here to protect you, and once you've had more practice, we can try a waking trance."

"I never knew it was so obvious to tell when I wasn't present in my own body."

"The only reason you can tell so plainly is because you are looking through my eyes. Human eyes cannot see

WHAT WE DRAGONS CAN. TO OTHERS, IT WOULD BE AS THOUGH YOU WERE SLEEPING."

"So, when I go back to my body, will I think I have something wrong with my eyes all the time after this?"

"NO, YOUR MIND WILL NOT REMEMBER THINGS AS THEY ARE NOW. YOU WILL REMEMBER THEM FROM YOUR NORMAL PERSPECTIVE. NOW LET US NOT WASTE MORE OF THE LITTLE TIME WE HAVE TODAY."

That was Vasin for "hush." He was always straight to the point and made sure we stayed on task.

"LET'S GO OVER SOME OF THE OLD LANGUAGE YOU HAVE BEEN WORKING ON TRANSLATING. THAT WILL BE SAFE ENOUGH TO DELVE INTO. NOW, I WILL OPEN A DOORWAY FOR YOU TO GO THROUGH AND ACCESS THAT KNOWLEDGE."

Before I could ask how he was going to do that, he closed his eyes, cutting off the outside world. It was as if I was being pulled along into his subconscious, a white world that seemed to go on forever. Then a cabinet appeared out of thin air as did an overstuffed leather chair.

"GRAB ANY ONE OF THE BOOKS IN THE CABINET. IT'S JUST MY WAY OF MAKING THE INFORMATION TANGIBLE TO YOU."

"Can I do this for you as well when we meld on my end?"

"IN TIME AND WITH GREAT MENTAL STRENGTH, I THINK YOU MIGHT BE ABLE TO ACCOMPLISH SOMETHING SMALL."

"So what you're really saying is 'no,'" I remarked, reading between the lines.

"WHEN IT COMES TO YOU, I WOULD NEVER SAY 'NO.' YOU ARE ALWAYS A SURPRISE TO ME. NOW, GRAB THE BOOK SO WE CAN GO OVER SOME OF THE THINGS YOU ARE STILL HAVING A HARD TIME TRANSLATING. REMEMBER TO STAY IN THE MOMENT WITH WHAT YOU ARE READING AND LET ME DIRECT YOU. IF YOU DWELL

TOO MUCH ON SOMETHING, IT WILL BRING FORTH THE MEMORY, AND I AM NOT SURE HOW MUCH YOUR MIND CAN HANDLE. YOU MUSTN'T FORGET YOU ARE IN MY SUBCONSCIOUS, NO MATTER HOW NORMAL I MAKE IT SEEM TO YOU."

"*I understand,*" I said, opening the cabinet filled with dusty old books.

I grabbed one at random but paused, seeing that one of the books shimmered as if it were glowing in the sunlight.

"*Vasin, why would one of the books be glowing?*" I questioned as I grabbed for it.

"*WHAT DO YOU MEAN? I HAVEN'T PUT ANY PARTICULAR EMPHASIS ON ANY OF THE BOOKS.*"

"*Well then, let's open it and see what your subconscious really wants me to read,*" I said as I sat in the chair.

When I opened the book and flipped through the pages, nothing was written on any of them.

"*Am I supposed to do anything special to see what's written in this book?*"

"*THINK ABOUT WHAT YOU HAVE JUST BEEN WORKING ON AND BRING THAT FOREMOST TO YOUR MIND.*"

I thought back on the entry of Miranda being asked to come to a meeting with the Crown. From what I'd gathered, Miranda had a close relationship with the ruling royalty. They worked together to make sure their lands were safe from outside kingdoms. Yet this meeting seemed different. Miranda didn't want to go, and in my last dream, she and her men were fighting over whether she should. I brought the memory to my mind and looked down at the blank page.

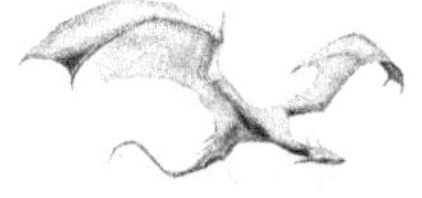

"Queen Miranda, how good of you to come. It has been ages since you last graced us with your presence," Queen Sarah said, kissing my cheek.

"Unfortunately, things back home with the clans have taken much of my attention," I answered carefully.

I knew she was mad I hadn't been able to make it to the last few social events with the royals and nobles from Errit. I simply couldn't stand going to them. I had way more practical things to do with my time than parading around in a flouncy dress. We had a tenuous relationship between our kingdoms, and I did as much as was required to keep things peaceful.

"How have you been, King Edmund?"

"With good health, two sons, and a peaceful kingdom, I couldn't ask for more," he answered politely, nodding at me in thanks for my inquiry.

"May I ask why Your Majesties have called this meeting? Not that I don't enjoy our time together... I just got the feeling there was something you wanted to talk about?" I ventured. If I didn't move things along, we'd be stuck in pleasant conversation for hours.

"Yes. We would like to secure an alliance with Errit in a marriage between our children," Queen Sarah said, beaming.

"That is wonderful news, but what can I do for you in this situation?" I asked, feeling a weight of unease in the pit of my stomach.

"One of the terms of the agreement is that your daughter would be married to our second son. They want to know that you and your people are at their disposal as you are with us," King Edmund answered.

I felt as if I'd been slapped in the face. Our clans had worked alongside the royalty of this land for generations, each respecting the other. In this one request, they had shattered years of co-existence. What made them think I would hand over my only child to be some bargaining chip? They may do things that way in their kingdom, but there was no way in hell I would ever force my daughter to marry someone she didn't love.

"Just to make sure I understand this correctly... you want Emery, my only child, to marry your son, she has never met, so our people can be at the beck and call of another kingdom?" I asked, trying to keep my composure, feeling my nails biting into my palms.

"If you need to say it in such crass words, then yes, that is the root of the request. I would, of course, make sure it was an appropriate situation for your clansmen to be involved in. Your daughter would also have the best care and education living here in the castle," King Edmund rebutted, waving a hand as if it was no big deal.

"I'm sorry, they would ask you for permission to use MY people?" I snapped, unable to contain my irritation at the flippant remark.

"Of course. They are my subjects as well. I'll want to make sure they are sent on a mission that will help our lands, not just fight a petty battle they might have with another kingdom," King Edmund said, leaning forward on his throne to look at me. "Do you have objection to this request from your King?"

Who the fuck did he think he was, calling himself "my king?" I was the Queen of the Mercenaries, not a lap dog to do tricks.

"With all due respect, you are not my king. I'm the ruler of my land, and my subjects are not under your control. I bow to no one, least of all you. My daughter is not some pawn for you to use to make a better deal for your coffers, Your Majesty," I growled out, feeling my face flush with anger.

I knew very well what I'd just said would be the same thing as declaring war on the Crown. Did I care... no, not really. I wasn't going to let my people be used at the whim of some royal prick who didn't even care about their lives.

"Do you realize what you're doing?" Queen Sarah asked, her face stricken with shock. "Apologize and bend a knee if you want any hope of returning to your daughter."

I looked around to see the King's Guard moving in, trying to surround me but still keeping their distance. I looked behind my five husbands, and guards were now flanking me. They all met my glance and nodded ever so slightly in understanding. I wasn't going to be taken prisoner to be used against my people. I would either make it out of this castle alive or die trying, and my men were with me all the way.

Not wanting to see any more, I pulled myself out of Vasin's consciousness and back into my own body. I gasped when I opened my eyes, emotions coursing through my brain at what I'd witnessed. I knew she never made it back to her daughter. It was the first memory I'd had of her, and one I wouldn't ever forget.

"Why do I keep seeing her?" I asked, cradling my head in my hands, trying to calm myself down.

"THAT WAS A MEMORY OF QUEEN MIRANDA, AND HER DRAGON WAS CHEERY," Vasin said gently, confirming what I already guessed—she was the Raven Queen. "IF I HAD KNOWN IT WOULD BE SO UPSETTING TO YOU, I WOULD HAVE TRIED TO STOP THE

MEMORY. ALTHOUGH I BELIEVE SOMETHING HAS TIED YOU TO HER. IT SEEMS SHE TRANSFERRED MANY OF HER MEMORIES TO YOU FOR SOME REASON."

"It's fine. I'm glad I saw it. I couldn't watch her men die there in the castle," I said, feeling tears prick the corners of my eyes.

"*FROM WHAT YOU HAVE SHARED, YOUR DREAMS HAVE MADE THEM REAL TO YOU. I KNOW YOU ALREADY LIVED THROUGH HER DEATH AND THE PAIN SHE FELT AT LOSING THEM. I AM HAPPY TO TELL YOU THAT HER DAUGHTER BECAME ONE OF THE GREATEST WARRIOR QUEENS THE MERCENARIES EVER HAD. THE MERCE-NARY WAY OF LIFE WOULD HAVE VANISHED HAD SHE NOT BEEN LEADING THE CHARGE. WITH THE DEATH OF HER MOTHER AND FATHERS, SHE VOWED TO AVENGE THEM AND IS REMEMBERED FONDLY, EVEN NOW,*" Vasin comforted, nuzzling against my back.

"What was her daughter's name?" Trying to connect the dots.

"*QUEEN EMERY, THE LAST REIGNING QUEEN BEFORE YOU. HER SON REIGNED AFTER HER BUT WAS KILLED BEFORE HE COULD HAVE ANY CHILDREN. SINCE THERE WAS NO BLACK DRAGON TO PICK ANOTHER RULER, THE MERCENARIES HAVE BEEN WITHOUT A TRUE LEADER SINCE.*"

"Cassarah, where the hell are you?" Cole called out.

"Must be dinner time," I said, rubbing my palms into my eyes to hide the tears that had threatened to fall.

"There you are," Cole said, walking up to us.

I looked up and gave him what felt like a convincing smile.

Apparently, it wasn't convincing enough since he kneeled in front of me, grabbing my face. "What the fuck are you crying about alone in the woods with your dragon?"

"Vasin and I were working on harmonizing, and I ended up getting pulled into a memory of Miranda... when they all died," I explained.

"Wait, the person you keep dreaming about?" Cole asked, dropping his hands after using his thumbs to wipe away my tears.

"Yeah. Miranda, the Raven Queen. This memory also showed me what started the Great War. King Edmund and Queen Sarah wanted to use her daughter, Emery, to sweeten the deal on an alliance with another kingdom. Miranda flat out refused their request and declared they were separate from the rule of the kingdom." I took a deep breath, trying to ground myself. "I stopped watching the memory because I didn't want to see their deaths again. Vasin told me her daughter led the revolt and saved everyone."

"So we finally have the whole story about what happened. Sal will be pissed he didn't get to find it first. Fuck, wait 'til he figures out you've had first-hand viewing of it all." Cole smirked.

I groaned, knowing I would now be required to write down everything I knew about Miranda. "Maybe I'll get lost on the hunt tomorrow, and we'll never have to tell him."

"That's the spirit. Come on, let's go eat before Helena sends out reinforcements," Cole said, holding out a hand and pulling me to my feet.

"Right, like Abbott is going to be much of a threat." I giggled, knowing what a softie he was outside of training.

Cole glanced over his shoulder at me. "You know you're the only person he acts that way around, right?"

I just smiled in answer, shrugging my shoulders. Cole rolled his eyes at me and kept walking.

"CASS, DO YOU THINK MIRANDA IS TRYING TO TELL YOU SOMETHING? I HAVE A STRANGE FEELING THAT MEMORY NEEDED TO BE SHARED WITH YOU, AND THERE IS SOME CONNECTION TO WHAT IS HAPPENING NOW."

"We'll have to try it again and find out," I said, giving Vasin a hug and a good scratch before I walked back to the house with Cole.

"Vasin seems to think there might be a connection between us," I mused aloud.

"You're going to be Queen soon, and we are on the verge of a war with the kingdom. Sounds like you could learn a thing or two from her," Cole said, glancing sidelong at me.

"We still don't know if I'm going to be Queen. There is still the job I have to survive before that." I sighed.

Cole stopped and turned on his heel, cupping my neck with one of his hands, causing me to gasp at his reaction. "You need to cut that shit out right now. As long as you don't fuck it up or die, they have no reason not to accept you."

"Great pep talk." I scowled at Cole, shoving out of his hold.

In the past few months, he and Abbott had decided I needed to learn to be okay with contact, so they had been much more free with small touches here and there than I would have liked. Brushing hair out of my face, sliding a thumb along my jaw, holding my hand... Cole, in particular, seemed to have a particular attachment to my hair, always tugging on it or playing with strands of it when I had it down. Although, I had to admit that having their attention in that way made my heart flutter and body heat.

"You don't have to be a dick about it. I was just trying to help," Cole grumbled as we walked into the kitchen. "Tomorrow will be a great chance to see where you still suck and need more work. That's the point of these hunts."

"When I was a trainee, I loved going on hunts," Helena chimed in as she set food on the table. "My first hunt was where I met your grandfather. He'd already finished his training, so we didn't get much chance to interact outside the hunt."

"I never knew that," Cole said, sitting at the kitchen table.

I grabbed the dishes and set them on the table before I sat between Cole and Abbott, knowing they would throw a fit if I sat elsewhere.

"Yes, your grandmother was quite the wild woman back in those days," Ballard shared, kissing Helena on the cheek before he sat with us. "She had aspirations of becoming the best mercenary in all the clans."

"I would have too if I didn't have to take care of you." Helena winked at Ballard as she filled our bowls.

"My parents had an arranged marriage, but I'd always hoped to fall in love with the person I was going to marry. Now with how life has changed, I'm not sure how all that'll work for me," I said, smiling at the thought of Ballard and Helena when they were young.

"Of course, you should fall in love. What fun is life if you live it all alone with no one to share it with?" Helena asked, making it sound like I should've already known such things. "Besides, once we get you crowned, the guardians will be selected, and you'll have your choice of men to pick from."

"Wait, what?" I asked, surprised by this information.

Helena gave me a disapproving look. "Child, have you learned nothing from Sal? Every king or queen selects men and women from all the clans to be their personal guardians. Many of the queens of old ended up marrying one or more of those guards. So pick wisely, my girl. They will be around you at all times."

Blushing at her words, I took a moment to wrap my head around the idea before speaking.

"I mean, I read about that tradition, but I didn't think it would still be practiced now. I'm not sure I really need them. I have Vasin to keep me safe and share my life with." I shrugged, poking at the food on my plate, not looking at anyone. I could feel both the boys stiffen beside me.

"No, no, no." Helena waved her spoon at me, catching my eye. "That is hardly the same. I'm talking about when you have the worst day imaginable, who would be the person or persons to hold you and tell you everything will be okay? When you have something to celebrate, who is going to dance with you in the kitchen of your home? When you find who you want to share the rest of your life with, you will come to understand what I mean. Life is never really lived 'til you have met your soulmate or mates and you live it together."

I had always dreamed of falling in love, but could you really love more than one person? Then my thoughts drifted to Miranda and her men. I'd felt the love they had for each other and knew she didn't love one more than another. They were devoted to each other equally. Was that something I was capable of?

"Enough, Helena, the poor girl gets it. She's never had the expectation of finding her soulmates. Do you really think her mother would have left that to chance?" Ballard said, patting Helena's hand to calm her.

"Hmph, I suppose not," was all Helena said on the matter.

I giggled at their exchange and glanced at Cole to see him watching me with an expression I couldn't quite figure out. I looked away first and dug into my meal as Abbott shifted so his leg rested against mine as we finished eating.

Sixteen

Time to Hunt

"Why does everything we do around here start before the sun is up?" I grumbled, rubbing the sleep from my eyes.

"You would think you'd be used to it by now," Becka teased, giving me a cheerful smile, her eyes alight with excitement.

"I'm going to need to sleep for a week when I'm done with training. Even that may not be long enough. If you wanted me to stay up 'til dawn, I could do that, no problem," I whined around a mouthful of porridge.

"It seems as though your ladylike manners have all but been forgotten," Becka pointed out, giving me a little frown of disapproval. "Besides, once you're done training, you're going to be our queen, and I doubt that will allow you much time to sleep."

I stuck my tongue out at her, not having the energy to argue over such things. I'd been doing my best to adapt to this lifestyle, and I was proud I could talk with my mouth full, no matter who complained about it.

"I think it's about time for her to finally loosen the corset strings," Cole argued, sliding onto the bench next to her.

"See, even he agrees with me," I said, stuffing another spoonful of food in my mouth.

Becka shook her head and tossed up her hands. "I give up. No one should have ever let you two become friends. You were both easier to manage when you hated each other. Just keep in mind, mister, I was her best friend first," Becka warned, getting up from the table.

"Hey, mouse, you in there?" Cole asked, tapping a finger on my forehead.

"Hmm, what?" I said, shaking myself back to the present.

"You've been holding that spoon up to your mouth like an idiot for the past five minutes," he explained.

"It has not been five minutes," I snapped.

"Whatever you say. Just don't get lost in that big head of yours when we're on the hunt. It could get someone killed," Cole chided.

"Don't worry, once I'm in the saddle, I will be more focused. I have a lot more to prove out there than any of you," I assured him.

"I'm just lookin' out for myself. I don't want the someone who gets killed or hurt to be me." Cole grinned as I punched him in the arm. "Come on, let's get our horses ready. We don't want to get left behind."

I tossed my bowl into the sink and followed Cole. When we got to the barn, I felt Cole's demeanor change immediately, his body stiffening and his hands clenching into fists. I peered around him to see what had made him so upset. Then I understood—Richard was back from his assignment.

"I see you're still on babysitting duty there, Cole," Richard said with a snide grin.

"What took you so long? I thought you said that assignment you went on would only take two weeks?" Cole shot back.

For some reason, I didn't understand—Richard and Cole were each other's nemeses. They had been part of the same group of trainees as Becka, yet Richard was the only one who had been unable to become an accepted mercenary. It had taken him an extra year for them to grant him his status, but he wasn't awarded the clan's crest. I learned this limited him to basic assignments, and he was barred from working on any sensitive cases, which pretty much meant he couldn't have anything to do with me. Becka told me he wanted to be considered for one of my personal guardians, but now that I understood what that meant, I knew I would never have considered him anyway.

"The job turned out to be a bigger task than anyone had anticipated. Bringing in a bigger haul for us, I might add," Richard taunted, very satisfied with himself.

"Richard, are you joining us on the hunt?" I asked, stepping around Cole to keep the situation from escalating.

"I would be honored to join you on your first hunt, Lady Cassarah," he said formally, giving me a little bow.

I raised an eyebrow at the greeting. "It seems you've picked up some courtly manners on your trip."

Did he think acting like this would win me over?

"Yes, m'lady. I hope someday to be of service to you and thought it would be best to know how to interact with a noble woman," Richard said, giving me what I think was supposed to be a flirtatious look.

I gave him a tight smile in return. "Well, shall we get our horses ready?"

I grabbed Cole's arm and pulled him along, not leaving a chance for them to talk further as I dragged him with me to Inali's stall.

"You can let go now," Cole rumbled, pulling gently against my grip.

"Why do you let him get under your skin like that?" I asked, whirling around and glaring at him. "You know that's why he says those things... he likes to see that he can upset you."

"I can't explain it, but ever since we were little, it's always been like that with the two of us," Cole said with a shrug of his shoulders.

I sighed and shook my head before I walked into Inali's stall. I would never understand him. Inali snuffled me as I brushed her down, checking to see if I had any treats in my pockets.

"Sorry, girl. I forgot to bring you something. I would forget my own head this early in the morning if it weren't attached."

Giving up on finding anything, she went back to picking at the bits of hay left over from last night. I headed to the tack room to grab my saddle and found Richard lingering there as if waiting for someone.

"Lady Cassarah, I have a message for you," he whispered.

"From who? Did my father reach out to you?" I asked, shocked.

"I know nothing about your family. It came from Queen Mary for you as Queen of the Mercenaries."

My jaw fell open, and I'm sure I looked like a fish gasping for air. "Wait. What? The queen? How did you meet the queen?"

"Quiet. Not so loud... this message is for your ears only," Richard hissed, stepping closer.

I searched his face, trying to discern what was going on. Why would Queen Mary have a message for me? I felt a knot of mistrust in my chest, making me feel that everyone in the clan was in danger.

"Crown Prince Gavin has been kidnapped, and she wants you to find him," Richard whispered quickly, his eyes watching the door.

"Richard," I said slowly, trying to get his attention.

When he finally looked at me, I held his gaze as I spoke. "How does the queen know I'm here? More than that, how does she know I'm to be your queen? Think carefully... these answers could potentially save or kill you."

If he'd in any way betrayed the clan, there was no saving him, but if he had a reasonable explanation, then there might be hope.

"My mission was to join a small group of newly hired groundskeepers in the castle to get a feel for what was happening in the capital. We knew the king was unhappy with Lord Everett and demoted him from captain to just a commander in the castle guard. Lord Everett had been pressing the king to make a swift and hard judgment on us mercenaries after we supposedly kidnapped you and the dragon. The king agreed with him but lost faith in him when he went against the king's orders and performed a raid of Royal City and killed any and all suspected mercenaries on sight," Richard said. He looked at the ground, unable to meet my gaze as he relayed the story.

"You're telling me that Lord Everett killed innocent people because the mercenaries supposedly kidnapped me?" I asked through clenched teeth, trying to keep my anger in check.

"Yes, m'lady, that's what I'm saying. After he did that, the king removed him from power, and he didn't take it very well."

"I imagine not. So how does the queen fit into all of this?"

"I was in the stable getting ready to send a messenger pigeon reporting back when the queen walked in. Her guards stole the bird away from me before I could let it loose. I'd used our code, so they had no idea what I'd written, but they still guessed who I was writing to," Richard explained.

"Did you tell the queen I was here? Why does she want to speak to me? I don't understand what this all has to do with us," I pressed, still not following where the story was heading.

"M'lady, it's no surprise to anyone in the castle that the owner of the black dragon would be anywhere *but* here. It may not be common knowledge to the rest of the kingdom, but the royalty still remembers the last war with the mercenaries. The queen knows. I'm sure that's why they thought about making you a candidate for the prince. They'd hoped to keep you out of our clutches and under their control," Richard said, tensing at the sound of someone walking by.

"That makes sense, I guess, but what did the queen want? Why would she risk talking with me?" I questioned, knowing that the window to hear this was closing quickly.

"They believe Lord Everett kidnapped Prince Gavin, and the queen wants you to find him and bring him back," Richard hurriedly said just as Becka walked into the tack room.

"Oh!" Becka paused, coming to a halt as she looked between us. "I'm sorry, did I interrupt something?"

I looked over at her and smiled. "Not at all, he was just telling me how my parents were doing. He wasn't able to talk with my father, but he was just sharing the goings on around the estate. I was asking so many questions we lost track of time. Let me grab my saddle, and we can be off."

"Okay..." Becka said, but I got the feeling she didn't really believe me.

I slid my saddle off its stand, draped my bridle over the seat, and headed back to Inali. My mind was bursting with the information Richard had just shared. Lord Everett wouldn't dare to kidnap the king's son, would he? If he had any hope of getting back in the king's good graces before, there was no chance now. Why would the queen think we would be willing to help find her son? We were definitely not on the sort of terms where she could ask for a favor like that.

"Vasin, do you know anything about the prince being kidnapped?"

The job I'd given Vasin while I was doing my training was to keep me informed of what was going on in our kingdom. He could communicate with all the other dragons in the land, and since they couldn't talk to their masters and tell them about us, it was the safest source of information.

"*There hasn't been a word of it through the dragon community, but I have not gone near the castle grounds. I shall head there at once and see what I can find out. I may not be back tonight. Even flying, it is a good full day's journey to get there.*"

"*I'll be fine. I am surrounded by mercenaries, and we are going deep into the forest, so the chances of anyone seeing us are slim. I doubt that anything will happen,*" I reassured him. "*I don't like that you're going to be that far away, but we need the information.*"

"Everybody mount up!" Cole called.

"*Be safe, Cass. I will be back as soon as I find out something.*"

I led Inali out of her stall and walked her out of the barn where the others gathered. It looked like there would be seventeen of us trainees and veterans combined. I shook my head to clear it once more before mounting. I *needed* to focus on the hunt for now.

Once everyone was ready, Cole and his mount shot off into the forest with us hot on his heels. After we had ridden for what felt like hours, judging by how much the sun had risen, Cole finally brought us to a halt and dismounted.

"Change of plans, guys. We aren't going on a hunt... not a traditional one, anyway. Today, we are going to 'play capture the flag, mercenary style,' " Cole announced as he pulled out two scarves, one bright red and the other sky blue.

"For you trainees, this is to test the level of your skill and see how you're progressing. The same rules as other mock battles apply. If an arrow is shot anywhere close to you, it marks you as dead. Likewise for knives. It shows your attacker had a clear enough shot that it could've killed you in a real situation. Once marked, the person is then escorted to whatever area you make as a 'prison.' You will stay there unless you are freed by one of your team members. Any questions?" Cole asked.

Abbott stepped up next to Cole when no one said anything. "This game will be a little different. We want to test how you work as a team but also the skills you have. So we are adding in that if you capture all members of the other team, that will count as a win."

"I'll be the leader for one team, and Richard will be the leader for the other team," Cole continued. "First, we will divide the veterans, then we'll split the trainees. I don't want to hear a damn word about us not making this a fair game."

I was surprised Cole picked Richard as the other team leader, but then when I thought about it, it made sense. This was becoming a challenge to see who could lead their team to victory.

To ensure everything was fair, Becka placed colored stones into a bag that each person would pick from. Once all the veterans had picked, then it was our turn. Since there was an uneven number of trainees, there was one black stone that would allow that person to pick their team. Lucky me, I was the one who picked the black stone.

"What team do you pick, Cassarah?" Becka asked when I showed her my stone.

I'd really hoped I wouldn't need to make this choice, but I was destined to make these hard choices in my life now. I closed my eyes for a moment and thought about what would be the most beneficial.

"I choose Richard's team," I announced.

Becka's brows shot up in surprise, and I could see Cole scowling behind her. Abbott even seemed to be shocked by my choice since he was on Cole's team too. But I needed to be able to do this without them. I needed to know I could handle things without them right by my side. I didn't know anyone on Richard's team well, and that would make this an even better choice.

"Very well, the teams have been decided. We will sound the horn when we have each reached a point one hundred paces away," Richard said, taking the blue scarf and waving for us to follow him.

"Good luck," I said to Becka as I led Inali to follow the others.

"You too. Keep your wits about you, and you'll be fine," Becka called, giving me a little wave.

Richard led us toward the canyon, so we had rock on two sides and caves to hide the banner in. Once we found a spot a hundred paces away, we staked the horses behind a stack of boulders so they were hidden from sight. We gathered around while Richard hid the banner farther in the cave.

"All right, team... we can win this one of two ways," Richard said when he joined us again. "We can focus on defending, or we can hunt. Which way do we want to win this?"

"I think we should defend. It will help our people as well as hone our skills," Brit, a trainee, spoke up.

"What's the fun in that? I say we really show what our team is made of and capture them all!" Gareth, one of the veterans, countered.

The discussion went around and around. No one could agree on which course of action to take. Richard just sat back and watched as everyone argued, not giving his input at all. I watched as our team grew more and more aggressive in their views. Paul got so frustrated he grabbed Gareth's collar, readying to punch him. This was doing us no good, and our so-called *leader* wasn't doing a thing to help the situation.

"Enough!" I snapped, standing up from where I'd been observing. "How are we going to accomplish either task if we're fighting amongst ourselves?"

At my words, they all stepped apart from each other, grumbling.

"Some of you veterans are acting no better than a trainee. If this is how you act on a real mission, then the fate of the mercenaries is grim indeed," I said, exasperated.

I paused for a moment, shocked at the words coming out of my mouth. How could I say these things to them when I was nowhere near adequate? All of them were looking at me with a mixture of shame and irritation.

"Well then, do you have a better idea, *Your Majesty*?" Kasper said, crossing his arms and scowling at me.

Did I? I wasn't even sure what the right course of action would be at this point, but we were out of time—the sound of a horn blew off in the distance. Cole's team was ready to start the hunt. We needed a plan *now* before they found us standing here twiddling our thumbs. Then an idea came to me, remembering one of the journals I'd been reading about past skirmishes the mercenaries had been involved in.

"As a matter of fact, I do. That is, if you would care to hear it. I wouldn't want to get in the way of someone more experienced, such as yourself. Let's hear your plan first?" I offered.

He cleared his throat and fidgeted uncomfortably. "You first."

"How gracious of you," I said, bowing my head slightly, knowing he was full of shit. "My humble opinion is that we do it all. Why should we pick one? There is more than one way to win the exercise, why limit ourselves?"

"Explain," Paul said, walking over to me.

"We have nine members on our team, they only have eight. We should use the extra person to our advantage. We have two people scout out the situation and steal the banner. Then we have two groups hunting the other team while one of us defends our banner. I know

Cole, and he'll go for the harder victory and the satisfaction of capturing our people. If we use this against him, then we have a chance."

"That's some tricky thinking there, little lady." Gareth grinned.

"We have four skilled mercenaries and five of us trainees. If we pair up with each other, that will give us experience and fresh eyes. The biggest challenge for both sides is being predictable. We're all trained the same way, and we all respond to things in a similar way. We need to change it up and use that very thing against them," I said, feeling excitement burning through my veins. "A while back, I was reading about this battle where they made a smoke screen to flush out the enemy hidden deep in the forest."

Owen raised his hand, and I had to hold back a smile when I nodded to him. "How do you make a smoke screen?"

"We use the horses. From what I read, they took green branches off trees, covered them in moss, and lit it on fire so it just smoked and smoldered. That way it doesn't set the horse or the forest on fire."

"Anybody disagree with this plan?" Richard asked, finally deciding to participate.

Everyone murmured their agreement and bobbed their heads.

"Very well. Kasper, you and Paul will steal the banner... no better thief than you. Dani and Brit pair up. Gareth and Maddox, you'll work with the girls to hunt down the other team. Owen, you stay here and defend the banner. Cassarah, you're with me. We'll work on flushing out the other team to make it easier for the others to hunt them down.

"To keep things interesting and unpredictable, I will not be leading this group. Cassarah, it was your idea, so I think you're the best one to make it happen. You said we need to be unexpected if we are going to win this, and I can't think of anything more unexpected," Richard announced, shocking me. But I didn't waste a second before taking control.

"Okay. Kasper, head out and only signal us if you have the banner. If you see the other team, avoid them at all costs. Your sole purpose is to stay undiscovered until you have your prize in hand, understood?" I asked, looking into Kasper's weathered face.

He was the oldest of the bunch that came with us and one of the most vocal about his disapproval of me being brought into the clan. I needed him to work with me on this and stick with the plan. He was our failsafe—if we all got captured but those two were still out there, we had a chance to win.

"I will do my part. Don't you worry your head, little queen," he grunted aloud before he set out with his trainee.

"We need to do this all on foot. The horses will give us away, and they are needed for this plan to work," I instructed as I drew out my plan.

Once I was sure everyone understood their part and what to do, we scattered into the forest, melding with the shadows. I tore off a sleeve of my white undershirt and tied pieces around my arrows, then tore off the other sleeve and every so often hooked a piece on a bush or tree, or under a rock—anything I could find to leave what would appear to be a frenzied trail.

Once I was out of cloth, I doubled back and met up with Richard, who had left his own trail. We climbed into the trees, shadowed by the branches thick with leaves. Now we waited to see what prey would land in our trap. Richard and I had positioned ourselves opposite of the paths we'd made. I knew the opposing team would think the trail was a setup and head away from it, thinking we were drawing them in. This tactic would most likely only work with the trainees. The veteran mercenaries would be much more cautious.

Sure enough, two trainees darted through the trees, pausing every so often to look for more clues. I nocked an arrow and pulled back the string, waiting for the perfect moment to strike. Once my target got close enough, I loosed my arrow, sending it to bury itself in the ground right in front of him. He was so startled, he skidded to a stop, falling backward in his attempt to avoid the arrow. Richard's arrow hit the tree by the other victim seconds after mine.

Two down, six more to go.

Richard and I each shot an arrow into a huge oak tree we had picked out to keep track of how many we had caught. We took the two captives to our prison inside a cave and tied them up to keep them out of the way.

"Nice shot," Richard praised once we left the cave.

"Thanks. It seems archery is the one thing I have a knack for." I smiled, feeling happy to be complimented by someone other than my teachers.

"Cassarah." I turned to see another group member, Dani, bring her captive to the cave. "Cole got Brit, but not before I managed to get this one."

"So, from what we know, we have three of theirs, and they have one of ours," I muttered to myself more than anyone else. "Those odds aren't bad at all."

"Yes, but keep in mind the ones they still have are veterans at this game. We need to be on high alert," Richard reminded me.

"Now would be the perfect time to use the horses," I decided.

This hunt was turning out to be way more fun than I thought it would be.

The three of us gathered the horses and tied ropes to their saddles, then to large branches. We gathered lots of dried moss off the trees and rocks, tying them to the branches. Once we were finished, Richard and I lit torches we had in our packs and set the moss ablaze. Horses, no matter how well trained, reacted to the sight and smell of fire, and ours were no different. They bolted off into the forest, dragging the fresh moss, which wouldn't do anything but smoke horribly for hours.

Richard, Dani, and I spread out and waded into the wall of smoke that the horses spread around us. Not only did it give us protection, but because we were upwind and had our faces covered, we didn't choke on the stuff. As for the other team, the wind blew it right in their faces, causing them to cough and gag uncontrollably, letting us find them quite easily.

I hoped the rest of our team remembered to keep their faces covered this whole time so they weren't affected by the smoke. This was the part of the plan I'd been worried about—if they didn't notice the smoke or hear the horses, then they would be in the same situation as the other team.

I came up silently behind a shadowed figure hacking uncontrollably behind a wall of shrubs. All I had to do was touch them with my knife for me to win. When I got close enough, I saw it was Abbott. That meant I would need to approach carefully. As I'd learned, he had a sixth sense—*feeling* other people near him. When I was within striking distance, I dove for the back of him, trying to go for a neck shot.

"Too slow," Abbott said as he dodged out of the way.

I tried to change my direction so I didn't land in the bushes and be fumbled up by them, so I hit the ground and rolled, getting away from him and back on my feet.

"Let's see what ya got," Abbott goaded between coughs, wiping at his eyes.

I realized that with my face covered and the smoke lingering in the air, he didn't know who I was. This I could use. If he didn't know it was me, he might not be able to predict my moves the same way he normally could. The downside to always fighting with the same person was they learned all your tricks. But that problem went both ways—I also knew his strengths and weaknesses.

Abbott was strong and smart, but I was faster, and sometimes that's all you needed to give you an edge. I opened my mouth to let out my own taunt but thought better of it. That would give me away, for sure. I bolted off toward the tree to his left—his weaker side—and ran up the trunk, flipping myself over and landing right behind him, pressing my dagger to the back of his neck.

"You dirty flying squirrel, I'll not go down that easy," he growled, grabbing my arm. He flipped me over his shoulder, slamming my back into the ground as I landed, staring up at the sky.

I heard him draw his dagger, going in for the kill, assuming he'd knocked the wind out of me. I waited a breath, then rose to meet him. I grabbed his wrist and flung myself backward, using his forward momentum to flip him over me and land with him on the ground, me sitting on his chest. This time I forced his dagger to his throat.

"Yield," I huffed as I pressed the dagger closer to his skin, almost cutting it.

"I yield," Abbott wheezed, relaxing.

Sitting up, I handed him back his dagger, but when I went to move off him, his hands locked on to my hips, holding me in place.

"Well done, Your Majesty." Abbott smirked.

I pulled down the cloth that had been covering my face, smiling. "How'd you know?"

"Cole is the only one who could've taught someone to flip off a tree like that, and he wouldn't teach it to just anyone. It's his hidden trump card that never fails to get him the win," Abbott explained.

The wind blew in our direction, kicking up more smoke and causing us both to cough. This time when I tried to get up, he rolled us over so I was trapped under him. His face hovered over mine, and his gray-blue eyes glimmered with intent. Slowly, he moved in until his lips brushed against mine, causing me to become frozen in shock. Then Abbott gave me a smile that made my body tingle at the sight of it.

"You've finally set that fire in your soul free. You should be very proud of yourself, little phoenix. You have overcome much to be here," Abbott whispered, making it feel far more intimate than it should have.

Shifting himself to his feet, he reached down, offering me a hand up as if nothing had just happened between us. "Come on, let's get out of this smoke and take me to your prison like a good captor." Abbott winked.

Shaking myself out of my Abbott-induced haze, I covered my face and headed off. When we passed by the designated oak tree, I shot another arrow to represent my new captive. It looked like we only needed to find one more to win the game.

The smoke trick had done it—we had been able to flush them out and turn the tide in our favor.

Back at the cave, I found four of my team guarding the six other captives, now seven with Abbott. Becka was in the group, her red hair all disheveled and full of twigs. Her face and arms had tons of little scratches like she had been attacked by a kitten.

"Becka, what happened to you?" I asked, trying not to laugh at how silly she looked.

"Laugh, I dare you. Once I'm free of these ropes, we'll see who's laughing," Becka snapped.

"In an attempt to get out of the horse's way, she jumped and ended up rolling down a small incline into a bunch of thistle bushes," Dani explained, trying to keep a straight face.

"Oh, wow, um... that sucks," was all I could say.

"Whoever came up with that harebrained idea is going to pay for it when I get my hands on them," Becka fumed.

My team all looked at me, then quickly away, not wanting to be the first to point fingers. I'd seen Becka mad before but never directed at myself, and I hoped it would stay that way.

"I'm guessing Richard is still out there since the rest of you are here," I said, clearing my throat and trying to change the subject.

"He said he wanted to go after Cole himself," Kesha remarked.

"I guess I'll go help him... see if I can't find our last captive as well." I sighed as I pulled my mask back up and ventured back into the smoky woods.

Out of the two of them, I didn't really know who would win. I knew Cole's skill, but Richard had a desperate need to win. I wouldn't trust Richard to play fair in a fight—he had too much to prove.

I kept low and ventured in the direction opposite of where we'd sent the horses. Knowing them both, they would want a place they could really duke it out with each other. I had a feeling this fight was one they'd been waiting to have for a while now, a chance to clear the air on who was better with no interference, but I wasn't going to let that happen. If I did, one of them would end up crippled or dead.

I came upon a clearing where I found Richard's horse calmly munching on grass. The ropes on the saddle had been cut, so he was free of the branches. When I stepped out of the trees to fetch the horse, I felt someone come up behind me. I grabbed my dagger from my belt and turned, slicing out at my opponent, but not before my feet were kicked out from under me.

Richard loomed over me, pressing a cloth to my face. I tried to yank his hand off, but as I struggled, the world grew dark.

Seventeen

Betrayal

Scattered dreams merged into nightmares as I struggled to wake up. It was like my body and mind were two different entities. I could feel my body being transported, but it refused to listen any time I tried to control it.

As I fought, there would be fleeting moments where I could move an arm or a leg, but then I was smothered with a foul-smelling cloth and was once again trapped, unable to do anything. Even though I couldn't move or see, I was conscious, and I caught snippets of conversation between Richard and whoever he was working with.

"Remind me why we signed up to do this job, Joss?" a deep voice grumbled.

"A hundred gold coins for each of us, my friend. Think of the life we could live with that!" another voice—Joss, I assumed—answered. "With this payout, we won't have to take another job for years."

"I don't like taking money from that head case who calls himself the Lost King. He's bad luck, you mark my words. Have you seen the way he controls people with that Birthright of his? I've heard if he controls them for too long, they lose their minds and kill themselves. I doubt we'll see any gold at the end of this that isn't covered in our own blood."

"You worry too much, old man. Have I ever led you wrong? All we have to do is get across the border to the place they plan to keep her without anyone seeing us. It's an easy job."

"Then tell me why there are only three of us for this part of the job? You saw the army he has. I'll tell you why... it's easier to get rid of witnesses when there are less of them."

Joss didn't answer, just grunted in response, and the men fell into silence once more.

Trapped in darkness with only three of my senses telling me what was happening around me, I had nothing else to do but think.

What possessed Richard to turn on us? Could he be working with this 'Lost King?' What did all this have to do with kidnapping me? How long has Richard been a spy among our people? This was too well planned for him to have decided on impulse.

Thoughts whirled around in my head as I tried to put the pieces together, but I was missing too much information. All these men were doing was giving me more questions than answers.

I must have truly fallen asleep because this time, when I felt myself waking, my body started to respond to me. I froze, hoping no one noticed I was moving. The wagon hit a rut in the road and slammed me hard against something, causing me to groan as my head pounded from the impact. My mouth felt like dried leather as sensations came back to me. I tried swallowing to wet my throat, but that just caused me to cough, making my stiff body ache even more.

Peeling my eyes open, I tried to raise a hand to rub my eyes, but it jerked to a halt before it reached my face. Blinking furiously, I tried to get my eyes clear enough to see out of. As I'd already guessed, I was in a wagon, surrounded by crates with my hands tied to the side railing. I lifted my head and found my feet also bound to the wagon. When I tried to get blood flowing back into my arms, a shooting pain ran up my arm as the circulation was restored. I gritted my teeth and let out a grunt as the wagon jarred my sore body. Taking deep, calming breaths, I gazed up at the stars and the full moon.

"Seems Her Majesty has finally woken from her slumber," Joss said.

I couldn't get a good look at his face with it cast in shadows from the full moon, but I saw enough to know he wasn't someone I wanted to be trapped with—stringy hair, broken teeth, and eyes that flashed with the thrill of seeing me tied up.

"What do you want with me?" I croaked out, knowing it was pointless.

Joss grinned, showing off his rotting teeth. "Now you know we can't tell you that. Besides, it would ruin the surprise, and we're almost there."

I let the conversation end, trying to think of another way to get him to give me the information I needed so badly.

"Where's Richard?" I asked. Maybe I could figure out a way to get information from him.

Joss looked down at me again as if searching my face for something in the moonlight. I kept my face blank, not giving him anything to go off of. I was falling back on my mercenary training before I even realized it.

"Oh, he's around here somewhere... Richard!" the man bellowed. "She's awake."

Moments later, I heard horse hooves approaching and saw Richard looking down at me. His eyes were hard as they met mine. This was a totally different Richard than I'd ever seen before. He had the look of a man who'd sold his soul and was happy to live in the darkness. A shiver ran through me, making me feel like I was back home—locked away, beaten, and starved.

"We should stop here. We are close enough to the border. We don't want to be found on the other side of the river," the third man said.

"That wasn't the plan, Penn. You agreed to take her to the location on Errit soil, hack off a piece of her to prove you have her, and return it to the mercenaries. Unless you don't value your life, then by all means, drop her off wherever. Just know I will have to tell the Lost King of this, and he'll hunt you down and use you for puppet shows at the next dinner party."

I gulped as I listened to Richard practically growling at them in irritation. So it was true—Richard was working for this mysterious Lost King. My mind whirled, trying to figure out how this information and them kidnapping and cutting off bits of me made any sense. What would the Lost King get out of this?

"I'm thinking if we keep going and cross the river, it'll be daylight by the time we get there, and the scouts on patrol will see us. We should stop and hide out for the day and cross at night," Joss suggested.

"Idiot. Who asked you to think? Now shut up and pick up the pace if you're so worried about getting caught," Richard barked.

With the snap of a whip, the wagon lurched forward, slamming me against a crate, my ribs taking the brunt of the hit.

"Shit!"

"Well now, that isn't very ladylike," Joss scolded over his shoulder at me.

"I doubt you've spent any time with a lady to know that," I taunted. Apparently, pain made me bold.

Joss laughed, tossing back his head. "Ho, ho, the little queen has some spunk to her, after all!"

"Joss, leave her the fuck alone," Penn snapped. "You're getting us in enough trouble as it is."

"Lighten up. What's the harm? Not like she is going to be around much longer," Joss said, elbowing Penn.

"It's bad luck to interact with the soon-to-be dead."

Before I could share my thoughts, the wagon veered to the right and sent me crashing into the crates once more. This time I tried to brace myself by curling my legs up as far as the slight slack would let me so they hit first. Penn hollered at the horses, cursing and trying to keep the wagon steady.

"Dammit! We've been pushing these horses for two days, and now he wants us to run them into the ground. We'll be lucky if we make it through the river before he crashes and kills us all."

I've been missing for two days? Vasin must be going crazy not knowing where I am. The drug must have cut me off from him if he couldn't track me down by now. Can I harmonize with him this far away? Should I risk it?

Deciding it was a risk I was willing to take, I closed my eyes and took deep, calming breaths. I fell into myself, reaching out to our bond's glowing connection. When I grasped it and felt it flicker, I knew I had Vasin's attention. I could feel he was reaching out to meet me halfway. Just as I was going to fully meld with Vasin, pain bloomed across my shoulder.

"None of that dragon voodoo, you little bitch," Joss snarled, waving his sheathed sword at me.

"Told you she was too quiet," Penn muttered.

"I was warned to keep you awake or knocked out so you couldn't talk to that black dragon of yours. I would recommend staying awake because you won't like how I'm gonna put you under again," Joss threatened.

Goddammit, Richard! He must have told them everything he knew about mercenary royalty and our dragons. When I got out of this, that fucker was going to pay.

Knowing I was being watched, I decided to try and fall into a waking trance. I'd never done it before, but Vasin had told me how useful it was to learn and gave me basic instructions on how it worked.

Looking up at the stars, I took in a deep breath, letting my mind drift as I tried to reach out to Vasin. I cast my mind wide, letting it stretch as far as it could. I knew the chances of reaching him this far away were slim to none, but I had to try. Just when I was going to give up, I caught a hint of something. It felt different than all the other times I'd reached out to Vasin, but it could be my lack of skill in this kind of meditation. It felt like an echo was bouncing back to me. It wasn't clear, mostly garbled so I couldn't pick up any words. I did get the emotion behind it, though, and knew I was heard and someone was coming. The echo became stronger as it got closer, but it still felt off to me.

"Hey, you awake?" Joss demanded, jabbing something into my side.

I quickly rolled away from him as far as I could and glared up at him. Satisfied that I was awake, he harrumphed, turning back to the front of the wagon. I could only hope I'd given enough information to be found.

"Shit!" Joss swore, standing up in the wagon to get a better look. "Is that a dragon?"

"Might be a scout from the border," Penn yelled as he pushed the horses into a faster pace.

Joss turned back to me, slamming his scabbard into my collarbone. "You little cunt, what have you done?"

I cried out at the sudden pain and force of the blow.

"You tell that dragon to back off, or so help me, I will end you right here, right now," Joss snarled as he slammed his scabbard into my gut this time, causing me to retch. Not having eaten for days, I thankfully didn't have anything to give up.

"No," I wheezed before Joss began to rain blow after blow down on me. I tried to curl into a ball, but the restraints wouldn't let me, so I twisted to give him my back. I could handle more abuse that way.

"You fucking bitch, I won't let you do this to me. I've come too far to see it ended by some cursed black dragon and his mercenary whore." Joss jumped into the back of the wagon with me so he could land his blows with more force.

A mighty roar filled the night as the air seemed to ignite. Heat seared against my skin, causing it to prickle with pain.

"Jump!" I heard one of the guys yell as the wagon began to shift wildly. The crates around me began to slam into me, and one rolled over my legs, trapping them. I screamed as another slammed into my back, unable to avoid it. Then the whole wagon began to shift to the left. The crate rolled off my legs and slammed into the sidewall, smashing through it. The rope around my legs jerked me down, causing the ropes around my wrists to bite into my skin.

The rope on my legs snapped under the pressure, freeing me to pull myself up to the front wall of the wagon. The knife I'd hidden in my boot was still there, and I managed to wiggle it free. My wrists were bound too tightly together to cut them apart, but I sawed away at the tether.

Once free, I looked out the front to see the horses had gotten loose, and the wagon was now careening right into the raging river. Learning how to swim was something I'd yet to master in my training. I knew in the pit of my stomach that without free arms and legs, there was no way I was going to live if I ended up in the water.

This left me with one option.

Taking a deep breath, I grabbed onto what was left of the sidewall of the wagon and tossed myself over it. Unable to do the move correctly with my limbs restricted, my legs scraped against the jagged wood of the broken sidewall, which tore through my leather pants and into my skin, making me grit my teeth. Tossing myself out of a swiftly moving wagon would definitely gain me a few good cuts from my less-than-skilled maneuver, but I did my best to avoid real damage, slapping the ground and rolling in the direction I hoped was away from the river. Finally coming to a halt, I landed facing up, looking at the sky as it began to lighten with the first signs of morning.

I'd made it! I survived!

My body screamed at the abuse it had been put through, and I could feel the warm trickle of blood as it ran down my leg. The wind whipped up a flurry of dust and debris, choking me. I rolled over, covering my face with my arms until the air settled.

I recognized the commotion as a sign of a dragon landing nearby. I could hear its wings settle back against its body, and even if I didn't already know, I would have been able to tell it wasn't Vasin. There was no connection, no bond. Just a hollow space in my heart, knowing he was so far away.

Now to pray that whoever this was would be a better option than Joss and Penn.

"Hey, are you okay?" a man's rough voice asked.

His voice was oddly husky like it had been overused or damaged and gone hoarse. I peeked out from under my arm and found myself looking into the most beautiful light green eyes I'd ever seen. They stood out against his dark copper skin, the likes of which I'd never seen before. When I didn't answer but kept staring, he gave me a gentle smile before reaching for the knife on his belt. Slowly, he moved over to me and cut the rope around my ankles.

As he bent over, I saw his hair or what I thought was his hair. It was in a style I'd never seen before. It went past his shoulders but seemed to be wound in tight braids? But that wasn't the right word for it. Gently, he took my hands, drawing them away from my body and cutting them free.

"Thank you," I said, sitting up and rubbing the raw skin where the ropes had been.

I kept watching him out of the corner of my eye. It was hard to tell anything about him from his appearance. He had on basic leather pants and a long-sleeve jerkin that were well worn, sharing no clues.

Then the red dragon approached, drawing all my attention. It lowered its head and took in a long, deep sniff of me, then snorted it out like I smelled bad. I'm sure that being in the same clothes for the past few days, unable to wash, hadn't helped.

The dragon surprised me by letting out a happy chirp, then a hum, butting the man still crouched next to me closer.

The man smiled and shoved the dragon's head away playfully. "I'm guessing by Tahir's response, you're the reason he hijacked me to come here."

Tahir hummed again, bobbing his head as if answering the question.

I reached out a hand, and Tahir extended his neck to put his snout against it in greeting. "Thank you for hearing my call, Tahir. You both saved my life."

Showing off, Tahir let out a puff of smoke and a chirp before he stepped back, giving me and his pair-bond some room.

"I'm Cassarah, by the way," I offered, smiling.

I decided to trust my instincts about this man and his dragon, seeing how they'd saved me.

"Jade," he said, returning my smile. "So what brings you dangerously close to the Errit border? Norden hasn't been on good terms with them for the past few years if you didn't know that already. Their border patrol would have killed you on sight."

"It wasn't by choice. I was kidnapped," I said bluntly.

"Why would they kidnap you?"

"I would love to know that answer myself. I can't for the life of me figure out how I'm connected to any of this or what it would do for them," I grumbled, heaving myself to my feet. I was willing to trust him, but not with everything. I wanted to hold some cards close, like being the future Queen of the Mercenaries.

"Right now, I need to find a horse and return home. I have people who will be worried sick that I disappeared."

Just as I tried to take a step and put my plan into action, I cried out as pain shot up my leg, causing it to give out on me.

Thankfully, Jade caught me before I kissed the ground. "You're in no shape to go anywhere with a wound like that."

Looking down to see what he was talking about, I saw a large wooden shard sticking out of my leg. "Well, that's not good."

Jade helped lower me safely back to the ground. "Let me grab a few things, and we can get you fixed up. You're lucky I was just coming back from a supply run for my village."

He rummaged through two large saddle packs on Tahir that I hadn't noticed before. The dragon also had a fitted saddle of sorts for Jade to sit more comfortably on Tahir's back. It gave me ideas for fitting Vasin with something similar for longer trips.

Jade returned with some bandages and a bottle of clear liquor. Using his knife, he cut up my pant leg so he could get a better look at the damage. I had a few deep cuts, but the major issue was the obvious shrapnel.

"You want a swig before I pull this out?" Jade asked, offering me the bottle.

I shook my head and closed my eyes. "Just go for it, but don't... *holy dragon balls,*" I screeched as he yanked the wood from my leg.

As I was trying to learn how to breathe again, he poured the liquor over the wound, causing me to swear like never before. Cole clearly was a bad influence on me. Jade chuckled as he cleaned up the rest of my leg and started to bandage it. His strong, sure hands made quick work of the task like he'd done this a time or two.

"There. That should keep it clean for now," Jade said, satisfied, but he looked at me with a pinched brow. "When we get you home, is there a healer nearby who can deal with this more thoroughly?"

Laying back on the ground, I nodded absently. "Yes, our clan has a great healer."

"Clan?"

Shit, shit, shit! Maybe he'll let it go.

"You're a mercenary?" Jade asked.

There blows that idea.

I opened my eyes and sat up to look at him, gauging his reaction. His eyes shone with something that made me relax and release the breath I'd been holding.

Jade pointed to the emblem on his necklace he pulled out from his shirt. "I'm of the Hell Hawks. Where are you from?"

From my lessons, I knew each of the clan's identifying symbols. Seeing the taloned foot holding a sword, I knew he was telling the truth as if the red dragon hadn't added to his credibility too.

Do I tell him the truth? Do I come clean? I decided to go for it. Just because I was part of Raven Rose didn't mean he'd know who I was. We were one of the biggest clans.

"Raven Rose clan," I answered.

"You are very far from home, little bird," Jade said, watching me with new eyes. I could see the wheels turning in his mind.

Not good.

"You thanked Tahir for coming to your call, not me. Did you really call him to you?"

I could feel my heart rate pick up. He was part of the clans, but Richard's betrayal was fresh. I wasn't willing to risk my life so soon after being on the verge of death.

"I was desperate, calling out to whoever or whatever would listen. I just assumed Tahir was the one who heard me since dragons have superior hearing," I rambled lamely, knowing my lie wouldn't work.

Tahir, not liking my answer, let out a low warning growl as he swung his head to look me in the eye. Jade grabbed my chin, forcing me to look at him when all I wanted to do was avoid his piercing gaze.

"Why are you lying, Cassarah? We're both of the clans, and we're on the same team. You should know better than to lie to any of us."

Taking a deep breath, I decided he was right. "I'm guessing my kidnapping has something to do with being paired with a dragon... a black dragon, to be specific."

"Did you just say *black* dragon?"

"Yes. His name is Vasin, and I can only imagine how panicked he is not knowing where I am, not to mention Cole and Abbott. Oh Lord, Helena is going to kick their asses for letting Richard kidnap me right from under their noses," I blurted nervously.

Jade snatched his hand away from me and sat back on his heels with a shocked look. His light green eyes looked at me like he was seeing a dragon with two heads that could talk.

"What?" I demanded, looking behind me, fearing that Richard might be coming back to finish me off. "Is someone coming? Do we need to hide?"

When I turned back to look at him, he was taking a knee, bowing to me. Now it was my turn to be surprised.

Unsure of what to do, I reached over and tapped him on the shoulder, trying to get him to look at me.

"Um, Jade? What are you doing?"

"I apologize, Your Majesty. I didn't know who you were."

"Whoa, what?" I exclaimed, flustered with his drastic change in character. "Jade, relax. Stop that, will you?"

Is this what it's going to be like when someone finds out who I am?

Now I was strangely grateful that my clan was harder to impress than Jade was. I wouldn't have been able to make any friends or blend in at all if they all reacted this way. Jade slowly sat back on his heels, lifting his head and meeting my gaze with a cautious look.

"Seriously, knock it off. I'm not your queen yet. I haven't even finished my training to be a full member of the clan," I huffed. "Technically, you outrank me right now."

Jade finally lifted his eyes to meet mine, full of curiosity. "How can you not be a sworn member of the clans yet?"

"I was raised outside of the mercenary life as a noble lady. When I pair-bonded with Vasin, Ballard and his team came to get me. I had no idea that my family came from a line of mercenaries until about six months ago. The clan decided I would have a year to be trained and make it through a job to prove I was worthy of becoming your queen," I explained.

"They can't decide that. The black dragon picked you, so it's a moot point. You *are* our queen... end of story."

I chuckled at his black-and-white view on the matter. "If only it had been that easy. I was on a training exercise when a fellow clansman betrayed me, then kidnapped and dragged me out here. I still haven't figured out how having the Queen of the Mercenaries hidden away on Errit soil does anything beneficial for the Lost King."

"I don't know anything about a lost king, but it must have something to do with the crown prince's disappearance," Jade said. "Lord Everett is blaming us, claiming it's retaliation for the mass killings he did in the capital. He's trying to get the king and queen to start a second Great War."

"How does that play into kidnapping me?" I still felt like I was missing something.

"Maybe we should check out the camp I saw on our way to you. It seemed like a large gathering of people, and there's no reason anyone would be in these woods," Jade informed me.

"Seems like as good a place to start as any."

EIGHTEEN

HIDDEN ARMY

"G uess I don't need to worry about you being scared of heights if you have a dragon of your own." Jade grinned.

I smiled, thinking of the last flight Vasin and I had gone on.

"Flying is addicting, isn't it? Come on, let's get you up."

Not waiting for me to even attempt to get off the ground on my own, Jade wrapped his calloused hands around mine and pulled me up so I could hobble my way over to Tahir, then he grabbed my hips and hoisted me onto Tahir's back. The heat from his hands lingered on my skin as he climbed up behind me.

"We have to assume they're part of whatever this plan is. They could even be holding the crown prince. Best to be ready for anything," I advised, trying to keep my mind off how he wrapped his arms around my waist, holding me steady against his chest.

"Trust me, Tahir and I are all too familiar with stealth missions," Jade whispered, his warm breath brushing against my ear, making me shiver.

If Jade noticed, he didn't comment, partly because Tahir bound forward a few strides before his wings lifted us off the ground, and the familiar sensation of flying took over. I could see the wide river slicing its way across the land, a stark boundary between the two kingdoms.

I thought back to the maps my father and I used for our lessons and battles. Where Norden was mountainous and lush with vegetation, Errit had deep valleys and harsher lands with poor soil. Errit made its fortune by mining the minerals found in the land rather than being able to use what was on top of it.

I couldn't figure out what good would come from trying to involve Errit. There had been no love between the kingdoms for many generations—Errit was always trying to push the borders to get some of our fertile land—but their army wasn't strong enough to battle against dragons, and ours was the only kingdom that had them.

"Look over to the left... see the smoke?" Jade asked. This time he was so close his lips brushed my ear. I jumped at the contact, causing him to hold me tighter.

"You all right there, little bird?" He chuckled, apparently amused by my reaction.

I was glad he couldn't see my face because I knew it would clearly show my embarrassment.

"I'm fine," I said, clearing my throat, trying to get the husky rasp out of my voice. "We should check it out. Can Tahir land in a forest this dense?"

"He'll manage just fine," Jade responded confidently.

As Tahir maneuvered for the landing, I was grateful for Jade's strong arms keeping me from falling off as we came to an abrupt halt amid the trees. As quickly as I could, I slid down Tahir's side, careful to land on my good leg. I needed to be free of Jade's arms. Tahir snuffled at me, and I absently scratched his neck behind his jaw, where Vasin always enjoyed it. Tahir hummed his thanks, butting his head into my hip.

"You have a way with dragons, little bird. I've never seen Tahir so trusting of another person before," Jade said as he came up beside me.

"Have you met many other people pair-bonded with a dragon before?"

"I've met my fair share," Jade said evasively. "Come on... the smoke was coming from this direction."

Jade's reluctance to answer my question intrigued me. The only other pair-bonded I'd met were at the hatching, and after that, I've never had the chance to interact with them again.

We walked in silence, not wanting to alert anyone to our presence. Cole had drilled into me the skill of walking stealthily, but it was much harder to do with a weak leg. Jade tried to assist me, but I shook off his hand. I didn't want to be seen as the weak link. I'd been working toward this for the better part of the past five months—to be an asset, not a hindrance, on a job.

Finally, we were close enough to hear the low murmur of voices. Peering through the branches, I was shocked to see an army of men sleeping. Some were huddled around fires, while others were wrapped in blankets scattered throughout the trees. I counted roughly about two hundred men from my vantage point. Some of the men had the hardened, tell-tale look of warriors, while others seemed to be wearing the threadbare clothes of street thieves and cutthroats.

Nothing about this made any sense to me. There had to be more to it.

Amidst the men, three simple pole tents were erected—two smaller tents and one larger one I would guess held the leader of this group of men. Just as I was about to motion for Jade and I to back away, Richard stumbled out of the large tent, falling to the ground. I could feel my anger flare at the sight of him and his betrayal of me and our people.

Following right behind him was a man I didn't recognize. He seemed familiar, but I couldn't place why I felt that way. His dark hair, sharp features, and deep blue eyes made him a striking figure. His clothes marked him as Erritian and had me looking at the men again. Sure enough, they all had the prominent clothing style of that kingdom.

"Why did you even bother to come back if you failed?" the noble barked at Richard, grabbing him by the front of his shirt and dragging him off the ground. "How could you have lost her?! Care to explain to me how you are going to goad the mercenaries into this battle now?"

"There was no way I could fight a dragon with those two idiot cutthroats you sent with me," Richard argued, pulling himself free of the man. "Henry, there is no way she survived the wagon crashing into the river... the bitch can't even swim. As long as she's dead, the plan will still work. They will retaliate once I give them the pieces of her body that I find. All is not lost. We still have your brother, and that is what we need to get your parents in the fight."

Henry's hand whipped out, slapping Richard across the face. "How dare you call me by my given name, you traitorous rat. You should be thankful I'm letting you live after losing such an important pawn. Maybe I need to be more persuasive next time to ensure the job gets done. It would be a shame to ruin you. You've become one of my favorite toys of late, you know."

Richard fell to his knees before the man, bowing his head. "I apologize. I spoke out of turn, My King. I am your loyal servant, and even without the power of your Birthright, I would follow you to Hell."

I felt my eyes widen as Henry looked down at him with a cruel smile. Then he lifted Richard's chin to kiss him soundly on the mouth, causing me to gasp. Jade slapped his hand across my face, covering my mouth before I made any other noise that would give us away.

"See that you don't disappoint me again. Now go find her body so we can finish the plan. Then I can leave this rustic shithole of a dwelling and be back in the castle where I belong. Too long have I been forced into exile," Henry snarled, turning on his heel and entering the tent again.

"My men to me!" Richard bellowed, waking up the men who'd been sleeping through the whole exchange. "Get your gear and head out. We have a mercenary queen to find, a crown prince to kill, a war to start, and a rightful heir to put on the throne."

I suddenly realized who Henry reminded me of—King Edward. I made to move closer to the activity, but Jade dragged me away from the camp and didn't let go until he thought we were safe to talk.

"Did you know there was an exiled heir to the throne?" I burst out. "How did he manage to get an army of men from Errit? How did no one know this was happening?"

"If the Queen of Mercenaries didn't know about it, why would you assume I have that information?" Jade asked, not answering my questions.

Flopping to the ground, I sat with my head between my knees, trying to process everything I'd just witnessed.

Over the past few months, I'd become so reliant on having Vasin around to talk through things that not having him was like missing a limb. With his vast knowledge, he understood the world better than I did. Heck, even Cole and Abbott would have been more helpful in this situation than I was.

"Are we going after the crown prince?" Jade inquired, cutting into my thoughts.

I looked up at him, searching his face, trying to get a feel for the man I hardly knew. He was a sworn member of the mercenaries, and he was pair-bonded to a dragon, but I was still getting a feeling there was more to him than I was seeing.

"What are your skills?" I asked, ignoring his question.

Jade stiffened for just a moment before he shook it off. His body relaxed as if my question hadn't bothered him. "I have many skills, little bird. Ask me what you really want to know."

My brows furrowed, not liking how he saw right through me. "Can I trust you?"

"Can anyone be trusted?"

"Stop doing that," I snapped. "Answer the question."

"I believe actions speak louder than words, and I would much rather prove to you I can be trusted. Now, are we going to save the crown prince or not, Your Majesty?" Jade asked with a little bite to his tone.

Apparently, he didn't like his loyalty to the clans being questioned. I didn't like pushing people, but this was no longer about saving myself and returning home in one piece. There was much more on the line now. If we didn't stop this, the outcome would wipe out the mercenaries and many other innocents along the way.

I rose to my feet and locked eyes with Jade, channeling the confidence that Abbott, Cole, and Becka kept telling me I had.

"Yes, Jade. We are going to save the prince and stop a war. You in?"

Jade's eyes flashed with something dangerous, and he gave me a toothy grin that would have worried me if I didn't know he was on my side. "Hell yeah, little bird. I'm all in."

NINETEEN

TO SAVE A PRINCE

I watched as fifty men followed Richard into the woods, leaving most behind to protect their Lost King. With only two of us and a dragon, it didn't seem like great odds, but Tahir could breathe fire, which evened things out considerably.

Jade was going to cause a distraction while I snuck in to see if Gavin was being held in either of the two smaller tents. It was risky, seeing as I didn't have two sound legs, but we had to make the best with what we had.

Tahir's roar sounded in the woods, and the sky lit up orange as he let out a burst of fire over the camp. The men leaped to their feet and scattered, trying to avoid becoming a human torch. Tahir made two more passes before he swooped down, grabbed two men in his clawed feet, and flew back up to the sky. Jade wasn't riding along on this attack—he must be hiding somewhere in the woods. I had to trust he would manage on his own while I did my part.

During the confusion, I slipped around the camp, getting as close as possible to the first of the smaller tents. They'd been pitched toward the middle of the camp so it would be easy to spot someone trying to sneak in or out of them.

Dashing forward, I kept low and was thankful the morning light was still low in the sky, the trees casting shadows. Reaching the tent, I didn't have time to check it before I dove into the open doorway and out of sight. It was filled with crates and barrels I could only guess would be filled with supplies. I couldn't see any sign of anyone having been kept in here, so I needed to move on to the next.

Just as I was going to slip out, I gazed at the bounty before me. This would be enough to keep these men fed and fit for weeks. Taking out their supplies along the way would definitely slow them down.

I thought about trying to get Tahir to set it ablaze, but I didn't want it to seem like this was a strategic attack. They had no idea who we were or if the dragon was running amuck on his own.

Peeking out of the tent, I saw a fire right in front with a cooking cauldron over the top of it. Zipping out, I grabbed a few logs that seemed to have just been put on the fire and hadn't caught all the way. Tossing them into the middle of the tent, the fire quickly took to the dry kindling of the crates.

What I'd forgotten to take into account, though, was that there were barrels of spirits in the tent as well. The explosion sent me flying across the camp, landing me right in front of the so-called *King's* tent. It took a few moments before I could gain control of all my senses after the impact. My hearing was muffled and my eyes blurry while my body seemed to move in slow motion. I rolled onto my hands and knees and headed in the direction I thought the other small tent was in.

"What do we have here?"

Before I could react, a heavy object slammed into the middle of my back, immobilizing me against the ground. Looking over my shoulder, I found someone's heavy, booted foot keeping me in place.

"Well, if it isn't the Queen of the Mercenaries," Lord Everett sneered, his lip curling strangely from the scar he got from Vasin during our last encounter. "I must admit, your kind does have a knack for being hard to kill, but like any bug, a firm heel can crush it."

This time, though, I wasn't the same helpless girl he knew. Twisting, I punched the back of his knee, causing his leg to give out and send him pitching forward, giving me enough of a chance to wiggle out from under his foot. Rolling away from him, I scrambled to my feet, drawing my knife from my boot, and crouched, ready for his next move.

"It seems the time you've spent lost in the mountains has taught you a thing or two. Now I won't feel so bad killing you."

"Like that stopped you from killing those innocent people in the city. I'll bet most of those people weren't even part of the clans," I spat.

Lord Everett tossed back his head and laughed, sending a chill down my spine. "You got me there. I slept even better that night, knowing no one felt safe from me. It was quite the rush." As if a switch had been flipped, the jovial mood he had been in changed to a hard, cold expression. "Now you'll learn firsthand how they felt."

Lord Everett drew his sword and advanced on me. He was big and powerful, but he didn't have the skill Abbott had. Lord Everett was all about brute force and the power behind his movements, which made it easier to identify his tells.

I ducked under his slash and dove forward into his space—it'd be harder for him to hit me with his sword with me so close. I whipped my knife across his chest, angling down toward the tender flesh of his stomach. He hissed in pain as he brought the butt of his sword up and slammed it down on my shoulder. The force of his blow knocked me to the side, but I managed to fall in a defensive crouch, barely blocking his next attack. A knife was not created to take hits from a sword, especially one wielded by such a strong hand. Twisting my knife, I unlocked myself and spun to the left, ending up behind him, back to back.

After taking a moment to steady my footing, I kicked back at his knee again, making him stumble to the ground, then slammed the hilt of my dagger into the back of his head, knocking him out.

I looked down at the man crumpled at my feet and knew I should kill him. If I let him live, then I was just giving him another chance to kill me later. I flipped my hold on my knife and grabbed his hair, lifting his head to give me access to his neck. Just when I was about to strike, I felt someone watching me. I looked up to be caught in the gaze of the so-called Lost King.

His blue eyes were alight with excitement as if he thought watching me kill this man was some form of entertainment. I paused, trapped in his gaze and the energy pulsing from him.

"Do it," he whispered. "He was weak enough to allow you the opportunity, so take it. Get your revenge because you won't have another chance, Dragon Queen."

His words brought forth a need to do as he asked, a desire to give him what he wanted. I needed to do as he said. I was happy to kill this man for him. It would make him so happy to get rid of this useless man who could be bested by a mere woman like myself. My Lost King should never have to suffer a man like this in his army. No, I would protect my king and stand by his side.

I could feel my hands moving, but I never let my gaze waver from the man in front of me. I would prove how loyal and valuable I was to him.

"*CASS! DON'T LISTEN TO HIM!*"

"*Vasin?*"

Hearing his voice in my head made me blink, cutting off my connection with Henry. Shaking my head, I looked down and saw that my knife was already slicing into Lord Everett's neck. Not very deep but enough to make him bleed. I tossed him away from me and backed away, panting, panic coursing through my body at what I'd almost done at this strange man's bidding.

I looked up and found Henry giving me a toothy grin. He knew how close I had come to succumbing to his will. He tried to catch me with his eyes again, but I did the first thing that came to mind—I threw my dagger at him, catching him in the shoulder.

He roared out in pain, his face contorting into something only a nightmare could conjure. "You little bitch, I gave you a chance to join me and spare your life. You won't be given that chance again."

Pulling the power of my Birthright forward, I gripped my bow and arrow, aiming it directly at his heart. "I won't need a second chance if I kill you first."

Effortlessly, I released my arrow, and it flew true from my bow, but another soldier jumped in front of it, taking it in the heart. More men converged around Henry like a human shield as he fled into the forest. Letting my bow dissolve, I turned back to the task at hand.

If we didn't save Gavin now, he would be lost forever.

Running over to the third tent, I tossed back the fabric of the entrance and found two guards' swords pointed at the crown prince, who was gagged and tied to the pole in the center of the tent. Gavin looked up at me with surprise and hope in his deep blue eyes. I could see the family resemblance between him and Henry, but Gavin didn't have the cruelty in his eyes that Henry did.

The guards seemed stunned by my appearance, causing them to freeze and gape.

"*CASS, I AM ALMOST THERE. HOLD ON A LITTLE LONGER.*"

"There is a red dragon, Tahir, and his rider, Jade, with me. They are friends of the clan, so don't hurt them. I need to free the crown prince before we can leave."

"I UNDERSTAND. WHAT DO YOU NEED ME TO DO?"

"Mind having an extra rider? Once I get Gavin free, we'll need to get out of here fast."

"OF COURSE. I WILL LAND AS CLOSE AS I CAN TO YOU."

"Who are you?" the guard on the right asked.

"The Lost King sent me for the prisoner. I am to take him to the second location in Errit to keep him out of the hands of our attackers," I lied, making the plan up as I went.

The guard on the left frowned at me, changing his position to point his sword at me. "Bullshit. There ain't no way that's true."

I shrugged my shoulders. "Worth a try."

Not giving them a chance to think about what I'd just said, I lunged at the guard on the right, whose sword was still on Gavin. Sliding in close, I stood right up inside the circle of his arms and used my hand to hit the nerves in his wrist, causing him to drop his sword. I snatched the sword as it fell and whirled around, slicing through his throat.

His warm blood sprayed everywhere, hitting me in the face and stinging as it got into my eyes. As quickly as I could, I wiped my face with my sleeve and switched the sword into my dominant hand.

The remaining guard looked at his fallen comrade and back at me. "You made a big mistake, little girl. You just killed my brother. I'll fucking kill you!"

The guard slashed at me, causing me to stumble back and almost fall over his brother's body. Jumping over it, I moved away from Gavin, who was struggling furiously with his bindings. The avenging brother bared down on me with a blow that would have taken my head clean off my shoulders if I hadn't gotten my sword up fast enough.

I needed to quickly find a way to get out from under his blade. My arms shook with the effort it took to keep the steel from biting into my shoulder as I desperately tried to figure out a way to get out of this situation. But I was trapped. I fell to my knees as my bad leg finally gave out after the abuse I'd put it through.

Just when I thought I was done for, a dark figure appeared behind the guard, grabbed hold of his head, and snapped his neck. Then it tossed the body away from me so his dead weight wouldn't smother me.

The shadows disappeared, and Jade stood before me, blood spattered over his features and mingling with the sweat on his face. His bright green eyes glowed with danger and the fever of fighting. Strangely, though, I didn't fear him as he held out a hand to me.

"You okay?" he asked in his husky voice.

I nodded, not yet able to form words while my adrenaline rush subsided. Just when I was going to move, the ground shuddered, and a loud roar pulsed through the camp.

"Get the prince and let's go. It seems your dragon just arrived."

"You're coming back with us to Raven Rose, right?" I asked, clutching his arm as he turned to walk out of the tent.

He stopped and looked at me for a moment, then bowed his head. "As My Queen commands, I will obey. I should warn you, though, I might not be very welcome."

His words surprised me. "Why?"

"A story for another time when we are not fleeing for our lives with a crown prince in tow."

I nodded, turning to Gavin, who was still fighting against his bindings. "Can I borrow a knife—" Before I could finish the sentence, a hilt appeared in front of my face. I looked over my shoulder and grinned at him. "Thanks."

"Try not to lose that one. It's a favorite of mine," Jade said with a wink.

Shaking my head, I turned my attention back to Gavin. "I don't know if you remember me, but we met once at the palace. I'm Cassarah, the pair-bond to the black dragon. I'm going to get you out of here. Try not to move while I cut you loose… they made these really tight."

Gavin stilled at my words while I worked at cutting him free. The knife was razor-sharp, slicing through the bindings easily. Once his hands were free, he worked on freeing himself from the gag while I got his legs free.

"Think you can stand? We don't really have much time," I asked, watching him closely.

It didn't look like they'd hurt him, but who knows if they'd given him any food or water. He didn't answer me right away but seemed to test out his limbs. Slowly, he pulled himself to his feet and wobbled a little. He almost fell over, but Jade caught his shoulders to steady him.

"Thank you," Gavin's deep voice said, filling the tent like I remembered it doing at the palace. "How did you, of all people, find me? How long have I been missing? Do you know what the hell is going on?"

I knew Gavin needed answers, but we didn't have a whole lot of time. "I don't know how long they've held you. I was kidnapped maybe two or three days ago at this point, but it was truly lucky that we found this camp."

Gavin opened his mouth to ask more, but I stopped him. "You have a lot of questions, I get that, but we need to get out of here before your brother gets his men in order and attacks us with purpose." I looked past him to Jade and signaled for him to help Gavin out of the tent.

Jade nodded and slung Gavin's arm over his shoulders, taking most of his weight. I made my way out first and headed right for Vasin. He was sitting back on his haunches, wings wide, snapping at the soldiers who dared challenge him. Tahir flew over and let out another burst of flame, scattering the men once again, giving us enough time to run to Vasin, who lowered himself to the ground and swung his head to me as I hobbled as fast as I could.

"Cass, what have they done to you?" Vasin let out another roar and gnashed his teeth at the daring men who came back to try their luck. *"I will rip them all to pieces for hurting you!"*

"There's no time... we need to get out of here. I have the kidnapped crown prince with me," I yelled over his internal roar when I reached him.

Vasin let out a low growl but listened to me as I helped Gavin onto his back. *"Can you take the three of us until we can get somewhere safer?"*

"Yes."

"Jade, let's go. You're sitting behind me," I instructed once I was behind Gavin.

Jade looked at Vasin, then back at me, as if he wasn't sure he should listen to me. Vasin turned to look at him and growled, letting his teeth snap.

"All right, I'll listen to your lady. You can put away your teeth now."

"Who is this man, Cass? I am unsure if I like him. He smells like death."

I tried to hold back my grin at seeing Vasin being overprotective of me at a moment like this. *"He saved my life, and he's also pair-bonded with Tahir, who is quite lovely. Let's give him a chance, hmm?"*

Vasin snorted and lifted his great wings to heave us into the safety of the sky.

TWENTY

THE NEXT MOVE

We flew in silence until we reached the other side of the forest, where a great open plain opened up. It would be far enough away from the Lost King's army and give us the advantage to see anyone coming upon us.

Vasin and Tahir landed right next to each other, each eying the other but not making any telling movements. Jade hopped down and pulled me off Vasin, then helped Gavin, who almost face-planted on the ground.

Seeing that Jade was dealing with Gavin, I walked up to Vasin and hugged his large head. Even though it had been only a few days, he'd already grown larger and his scales thicker. His head was almost as big as I was, making it harder to hug his snout. Seeing him next to Tahir made me realize how much bigger he was than a typical dragon. Tucking his wings away, he crooned and nuzzled my stomach as I scratched his eye ridges.

"I am really glad to see you," I whispered to Vasin as I fought against the tears welling up in my eyes. "I was so scared, and I didn't have you watching over me."

"DON'T EVER DO THAT TO ME AGAIN, CASS. I COULDN'T FIND YOU ANYWHERE. I HAVE BEEN FLYING ALL OVER THE MOUNTAINS LOOKING FOR YOU."

"I was drugged with something that kept me in this strange state where I couldn't control anything, mind or body. As soon as I could, I called out to you, but I wasn't sure if you heard me."

"IT WAS LONG ENOUGH FOR ME TO LATCH ONTO YOUR END OF THE BOND AND FOLLOW IT TO YOUR LOCATION. IF YOU HADN'T BEEN DRUGGED, I WOULD HAVE FOUND YOU SOONER."

"I know, I don't have any doubt about that. We're back together, and that's what really matters." Stepping back, I pulled my emotions together, ready to deal with the matters at hand. "Tell me what's been happening back home. Do they know about Richard?"

"YES, THEY KNOW HE TOOK YOU, BUT NOT WHY."

"I can't say that I truly know the reason either. I have far too many questions about this whole thing and not nearly enough answers," I said with a sigh.

"Um, Cassarah... are you having a conversation with your dragon?" Gavin asked.

"Yes. Vasin is filling me in on things I've missed since being kidnapped," I answered, forgetting people outside the clans didn't know this about the black dragon.

Looking behind me, I found Gavin sitting on a blanket, resting against a boulder and giving me a curious look as he munched on something. Tahir was settled on the other side from where Vasin and I were, watching our backs. Jade walked up and handed me some dried meat and a flask of water. My stomach rumbled, reminding me it had been a few days since I'd eaten anything.

"Thank you," I said, and he just nodded in response, not meeting my gaze. I wanted to ask him what was wrong but thought better of it.

"Sit and rest, Cass. We have a little while before we need to move on. Eat something to keep up your strength. We have a long flight back to the clan. They have gone into hiding and called a meeting of the clans."

"What? They went into hiding?"

"Makes sense," Jade said, drawing my attention.

"Why don't I know about this? I didn't even know we had a secondary location to hide out at!"

"If you are not yet crowned queen, then you wouldn't. In each clan, there are only five people who know the location… it's our last haven in times of trouble. I'm sure they would have told you once they could, but as you see, not everyone can be trusted," Jade pointed out, making me feel less irked about the whole thing.

"I know where they have gone. I can take you to them, but I'm not sure how they will feel about the crown prince knowing. What do you plan to do with him?"

"I need to find out what he knows before I can let him go. He might know more about why we were kidnapped since he was held longer than I was. Plus, this crazy Lost King is his half-brother."

"Very well, I will scout the area with Tahir while you get your answers. I will alert you if there is any danger."

"Thank you," I said aloud, then backed up to give him room to take flight.

Once Vasin was in the sky with Tahir, I sat and wolfed down my meat. My stomach now pacified, I sipped my water and observed Gavin. His face was drawn, and he looked tired with dark circles under his eyes. His once clean clothes were tattered and stained from travel and sleeping on the ground. He looked nothing like the man I'd met so many months ago in the castle's drawing room.

"Hey, you doing all right?" I asked as he stared down at his hands, running a finger across the rope burns on his left wrist.

Gavin looked up at me, blinking a few times as if coming back to the present. "Yeah... just a little rattled. First time being kidnapped and all."

I grinned a little at that. "This is my second time. It gets easier with practice."

Gavin looked up, shocked at my words. Then when he saw my grin, he smiled.

"Did you know that you had a half-brother?" I asked.

"No, that was a surprise to me. My father has never mentioned anything about a bastard born in our family. Guessing at how old he is, it happened before he married my mother."

"Did Henry say anything to you about why he was doing all this? I know he wants to be king, but that doesn't explain involving Errit and the mercenaries."

"He doesn't just want to be king of Norden, he wants to be king of it *all*. His goal is to wipe out any resisting force and conquer anything he can," Gavin said, shivering at the idea. "Did you see what his Birthright is?"

My mind flashed back to the moment I held Lord Everett's life in my hands and the need I felt to prove myself to Henry. "Some kind of mind manipulation."

"He can convince you to do anything for him if he can latch onto your mind long enough. I heard the guards say when he controls someone for too long or makes them do something too awful, it breaks them, and they become a drooling simpleton," Gavin explained. "My Birthright isn't quite as controlling as his. Mine just makes you feel comfortable enough around me to tell me more than you normally would. Sometimes I can't even control when mine affects people. He would leave someone in the tent with me if he wanted information from them."

"That is a very good ability to have around if you're trying to rule the world," Jade commented from where he was lying with his hands tucked behind his head, eyes closed. I thought he had been sleeping but apparently not.

"Okay, that might explain why he kidnapped you but wanted to kill me. My Birthright doesn't work that way... it's a physical ability," I mused.

"You're forgetting one thing you control that no one else can... an ability to access unlimited knowledge. If he had been able to control your mind and weakened you enough, he could've had control of Vasin too," Jade said, causing me to feel sick to my stomach.

"Holy hell, you're right," I swore. "He almost had me too. If Vasin hadn't come and yelled at me, I would've been putty in his hands."

Jade sat up and pinned me with his pale green gaze. "Don't sell yourself short. I saw you fighting him every step of the way. I don't think you were as close to giving in as you think."

"What's he talking about?" Gavin frowned, looking between me and Jade.

"Right now, I think it's better that you don't know. If Jade is right, then we are in way more trouble than I thought." I sighed, letting my shoulders slump. "We need to bring him with us, Jade. We can't let

Henry get a hold of him, but I don't know how the clans will take the crown prince showing up at our super-secret hideout."

Jade stood up and let out a loud whistle. "You're the queen, and there's nothing they can do about it."

"You keep forgetting that I'm not queen yet. I haven't finished my training or gone on a job."

Jade just looked, his eyes searching as they washed over me. I tried not to fidget under his scrutiny, but it was hard when my body started to heat under his gaze. "Let me worry about that. First, we must get to our clansmen and warn them about what's going on."

As I watched Vasin and Tahir coming back toward us, I had to agree with him. This was much bigger than the two of us could handle, even with our dragons. We needed the minds of our people, and if this was going to turn into the next Great War, we were going to need everyone.

"Do I get any say in this? I am the crown prince of this kingdom," Gavin asked, his frown now a full scowl.

"Not really, Your Highness," Jade said with a mocking tone. "Unless you would like us to leave you here to fend for yourself, then by all means, stay at your leisure. My guess is you wouldn't last the day before Henry and his men found you again. Who's to say if they will let you live this time or not?"

"Enough, Jade, no need to be cruel," I snapped.

Jade just shrugged his shoulders and started packing things back up in Tahir's saddlebags.

I walked over to Gavin and dropped down next to him. "Oddly enough, I've been in a somewhat similar situation where I had to make a choice to leave behind the life I knew for something completely unknown. I can't promise much, but what I can promise is that you will be safe, and I will do my best to get you back home. Protecting you will protect my people as well. You have no reason to trust me, but I hope you will."

As Gavin mulled over my words, watching me intently, I could feel a strange, warm breeze running over my body. I stiffened at it because it reminded me of how I felt when Henry was trying to control me.

"Gavin, are you trying to use your Birthright on me?" I asked.

"How did you know?"

"I could feel it tugging on my emotions. Almost like with Henry."

As soon as those words came out of my mouth, the warm breeze stopped and dropped away. "I'm sorry. I never meant to manipulate you. It's become a reflex when I'm unsure about something."

"No harm done. Just know I'll be able to tell if you try it again," I said, giving him a smirk. Standing, I held out a hand for him. "Come on, Vasin says we have a long flight ahead of us."

Walking over to Vasin, I brushed my hand along his glimmering black scales that had been warmed in the sunlight. I was steeling myself for what came next. I had to trust my instincts on this. I'd thought that my dreams were showing me a way to fix things between Norden and the mercenaries, yet I was discovering that wasn't the case. What it showed me was the life of one of the greatest mercenary queens we ever had to learn from. Now I was going to have to take all that knowledge and make the best of it.

"So you have decided to take him with us?"

"Yes, I've discovered some things that make him more of a risk to us if we were to let him go. Keeping him safe is the best choice, not only for him but for our people."

"Very well, I trust you, Cass."

"Only time will tell."

To be continued in Dragon Queen

ABOUT AUTHOR

Elizabeth is originally from Illinois but is now living in sunny Phoenix, Arizona. Though she is newer to publishing, Elizabeth has been writing for nine years. She started in YA Fiction but recently found herself loving the Reverse Harem genre. Like her favorite books, Elizabeth loves to write about strong women of all varieties. Not all strength is flashy or apparent at first glance—some lie just under the surface.

Don't Miss Out!
Be the first to know what is coming next by following Elizabeth's social media! You never know when or what will be coming next!
Website & Socials found here:

Also By

Mercenary Queen – Complete Series
Birthright
Dragon Queen
The Forgotten Throne
The Final Battle

Sunshine & Rainbows Omegaverse
Bailey-Rose Duet - Clouds & Daydreams + Petals & Promises
Lyra Duet – Knot Now Knot Ever

Omega Assassin - Complete series
Book 1 - Dual Nature
Book 2 - Hidden Nature
Book 3 - Perfect Nature

Knot All Omegaverse
Knot All Is Lost: Part 1 & Part 2 (Complete)
Knot All Is Ruined: Part 1 & Part 2 (Complete)

Caprioni Queen – Complete Series

Book 1 – Glitter & Guns

Book 2 – Blood & Heartache

Book 3 – Revenge & Truth

Book 4 – Love & Power

Gun Runner Princess

Book 1 – One For The Money

Standalone Books

Nicolette: Ladies of the MC

Lying Lainey: Underground Omega Syndicate

Hidden Empire Series – Complete series

Book 1 - Two Tricks

Book 2 - Three Tricks

Book 3 - Four Tricks

Book 4 - More Tricks

Book 5 - Our Tricks

Hidden Empire Novel

(SUGGESTED TO BE READ AFTER FOUR TRICKS)

Harper's Renegades

9 798889 580492